The Growing Season

Sanderson Ridge Book 1

Alicia Hitchcock

SUMMER

"It's not summer until the cricket sings."

Greek proverb

Chapter 1

Early morning sunshine peeked through the blinds, and magpies warbled in the trees nearby, drawing Angela out of bed. This was her favourite time of year. She'd always felt more optimistic in summer, as if the warm weather engaged a sanguine part of her brain that hibernated during winter months. She made a breakfast smoothie, then sat on the bench on the front verandah that faced the park opposite her modest home in the leafy Perth suburb. She flicked a 'good morning' text to Andy, then listened to a motivational podcast, hoping to absorb some of the confidence the speaker oozed. Giving the pitch of her career to BCG Corp, Mosaic Media's newest and biggest client, would put her on the fast track to a senior partner position. If Kyle hadn't given her the marketing internship when she'd moved to Perth twelve years ago, who knows where she might have ended up? She was glad to have found a career that incorporated so many things she loved, but there were still stressful aspects to it. She drank the last of her smoothie and checked her phone. No reply from Andy. It was unusual, but it was his last day of R & R before he flew back to the mine up north. Maybe he was enjoying a sleep-in? Angela took one last look at the birds flitting around in the gum trees, then went inside to get ready for work.

Every chair at the boardroom table was full, and all eyes were on her. With sweaty palms and a palpitating heart, she clicked start on the presentation. She'd pitched plenty of times over the years, but never to a client as huge as BCG Corp. The CEO and his top executives sat stony-faced, arms crossed, a palpable tension hanging in the air. Their approach was not uncommon. Even if they were already planning on outsourcing their marketing and public relations to Mosaic, they wouldn't want to appear too eager and lose the potential to negotiate their contract. Angela straightened and steeled herself, then went to the front of the room to present. Thirty minutes later, pitch complete and nerves dissipated, she sat back and listened as Kyle took BCG through the rest of their client slide deck.

When the executives had left the room, Kyle turned to face Angela.

'I think we've got them. It looks like that senior partner role might be closer than you think,' he said, before giving her two thumbs up and heading out the door. Angela glanced around, making sure the room was clear before she pumped her fist and silently congratulated herself. She'd worked hard on this pitch, and she was among the longest-serving employees at the company. She deserved this promotion.

She breezed out of the boardroom and almost ran into Paul, the finance officer.

'I hear the pitch went well. Congratulations,' he said. 'We'll have to discuss your options should things keep progressing.' He smiled at her, and she thanked him. She didn't have time to dwell on her achievement right now. She needed to send the pitch deck to the BCG team and get started on the storyboard for the photo session she'd booked for another client. She pushed through until 5 pm. On her way home, she drove her SUV through the traffic, stopping at the shops to pick up a bottle of wine and a pre-packaged lasagne for one. It had been a day worth celebrating.

Saturday mornings meant a luxurious sleep-in, undisturbed by the alarm. Angela peeled herself out of bed and checked her phone while she made a breakfast smoothie. She'd tried to call Andy last night, but he hadn't answered. She was starting to worry, but she couldn't do much about it. Reception at the mine was dodgy sometimes. Slipping into her gym clothes, she grabbed her drink and headed across the road to the park. The sun was already high in the sky, and the heat was starting to set in. It was best to get a walk in before it got too hot.

Her phone buzzed. She smiled when she saw Andy's name and the selfie she'd taken last week of them together on Matagarup Bridge. He would be eager to hear how her pitch turned out.

'Guess what?' She didn't wait for a reply. 'The pitch went so well that BCG wants me to be their account director. Kyle was thrilled with the outcome. I think I'll get the promotion.'

'That's great,' Andy said, his voice monotone. Angela's smile faltered. Andy was on night shift this swing. Perhaps he was tired. 'Listen, Ang, we need to talk.' She found a bench and sat down, stomach knotting. She knew what those words meant. They'd only been dating for six months, but Angela thought Andy was husband material. She was 30, but her biological clock was ticking. She'd already imagined their wedding in King's Park and then a little bundle of joy coming along nine months later. It was all going to be perfect—perfect job, perfect house, and perfect family.

'I wanted to do this in person, but I just...I need to do it now.' Angela's throat constricted, and she struggled to swallow. 'So, uh..., you're great and all, but I don't think this is working out.' Angela's throat made a choking sound.

'But Andy—'

'Sorry, Ang. I've gotta go. Bye.' She sat gobsmacked, world spinning, mind racing. How could he do this? And over the phone, too. Didn't the last six months mean anything to him? Hadn't he thought about their possible future together? And why was this affecting her so much? Was it because she'd actually let her guard down and fallen for him too quickly and too hard? She wiped her tears away as a group of joggers ran past. Then she stood and ran back home, avoiding eye contact with anyone she passed. Adam's car was in the driveway and he stood at her front door, hand poised to knock.

'Hey, how are you?' Adam said. She looked at him, lip quivering, and her eyes blinking back tears. 'Are you alright? What's going on?'

'Andy just broke up with me...over the phone.'

'He what? What a douchebag!' Angela stayed silent, and Adam pulled her into his arms. 'Angela, you're an absolute catch. You're gorgeous, funny, and intelligent. Plus, you've got a great job and your own house. Seriously. You can do way better than him.'

'I know. It's just...I thought it might go somewhere. I had plans.'

Adam shook his head. 'You and your plans. How about some retail therapy? It always helps me after a breakup.' Angela shook her head. She wasn't in the mood to be around crowds of shoppers. 'Well, call me if you need me.' Angela waved as Adam drove off. They'd been friends since she'd met him on her first day in Perth. He'd shown her around the share house she'd rented a room in and introduced her to their housemate, Lauren. The three of them still caught up together occasionally. But Angela and Adam had always had a closer connection. They'd shared laughter and tears, holding each other up through twelve years of whatever life threw at them.

Angela left her phone on the bench while she took a shower. With water running down her back, she closed her eyes and felt herself relax. Then she let her tears roll freely down her cheeks and her mind turn over her feelings. She knew she'd get over Andy, but right now, she needed to purge the disappointment and frustration. Was her reaction because she'd loved Andy, or was it that her plans had been derailed? She pushed the air out of her lungs and tilted her head under the running water, letting everything fade.

Feeling less fragile after her self-care session, Angela curled up on the lounge, ready to binge-watch her favourite small-town drama. Hours later, stomach pangs sent her to the kitchen. She grabbed a salad and then picked up her phone to scroll and saw one missed call from her brother-in-law, Kane, three missed calls from her best friend, Kit, and six missed calls from her little sister, Charlotte. Her whole body froze, and dread settled like a rock in the pit of her stomach. Charlotte answered on the first ring.

'What's going on? Is everything alright?' Angela asked. The phone was silent before a sob escaped Charlotte's throat, followed by her sucking in her breath before bursting into tears. Angela's stomach clenched. 'Lottie! What's wrong? Tell me what's going on?' Charlotte choked back her tears and tried to settle her breathing.

'They're...gone. I can't believe it. It's not...'

'Charlotte! What is going on?' Angela demanded. 'Put Kane on the phone now.' Charlotte's husband, Kane, came on the line. His voice was low and sombre.

'Hey, Ang. I'm sorry to have to tell you this. Your mum and dad have been killed in a car accident.' Angela couldn't compute Kane's next words as the room spun around her. This couldn't be happening. She'd fallen asleep, and this was a nightmare. It wasn't real. They couldn't be dead. She'd spoken with them a few days before. Her mum had told her about the new quilt she was sewing, and her dad had been fixing the tractor again. They couldn't be dead. They just couldn't. 'Ang, are you there?' Kane asked.

'Yes, I...it's just...' Tears welled in her eyes, blurring her vision, as she struggled to articulate her emotions. She didn't even know what she was feeling. Numbness settled over her, making even breathing a task.

'I know. It's bloody terrible. I'm so sorry. Do you think you can come back to the Ridge?'

'Of course. I'll pack a few things and head off now.'

'No, you're upset. Don't risk driving right now. Wait until tomorrow morning,' Kane suggested. Angela agreed to wait, but she knew she wouldn't get any sleep that night. She hung up the phone and let her gaze fall to the floor in front of her. Her parents were gone. She'd never see them again. It was only her and Charlotte now. They were orphans. Angela jolted at the sound of her ringtone. She knew it was Kit before she even looked at the screen.

'Hey, hun. I heard what happened. I'm so sorry.' Kit choked back a sob. 'Your mum and dad were the best. They've been like my second parents. How are you holding up?'

'I don't know. It doesn't feel real.'

'Yeah, I understand. You're coming back tomorrow, aren't you?' Angela made a sound. 'Okay. I'll see you when you get here. Drive carefully. Love you, chickee.' Still numb, Angela moved on autopilot. She turned off the TV and then called Kyle and explained the situation. He'd been so sincere that it had almost sent her into a fit of sobbing. She group dialled Adam and Lauren. They offered to come over, but she knew she needed time alone to process the news. Kane had been right about not driving straight back to the Ridge. She threw some clothes into a suitcase and hauled it next to the front door, along with some snacks and water bottles. Emotionally and mentally drained, she collapsed onto her bed, tears soaking the pillow as she drifted into a restless sleep.

Lying in the dark, waiting for her alarm, the realisation of what had happened hit her anew. She'd barely slept a wink all night. A deep weariness settled into her limbs, and her mind felt foggy, like trying to think through cotton wool. She rose and made herself a cappuccino in a travel mug. Sanderson Ridge was hours away, and she needed to make a start on the long drive. She barely took any notice of the changing landscape as she left the city and made her way through the rolling hills and the wide open plains to the small town of Sanderson Ridge, nestled in the middle of Western Australia. She knew it was going to be a tough drive, but she wasn't prepared for how many times she'd have to pull over because her tears were blocking her vision.

When the mountain range that formed a backbone for the town came into view, Angela's heart lurched. She had been meaning to come back to visit her family and friends, but life seemed to get in the way. With an array of new clients coming on board, she'd often worked 60-hour weeks. And for the last few months, her world had increasingly revolved around Andy. She balked at the thought of him. In the space of a phone call, she'd gone from despairing over her failed relationship to not caring if she never thought of him again. Life was too short and too precious to worry about things we couldn't change.

Kane's car was in the driveway when she pulled up outside the weatherboard home on Ridgeview Station that had been in her family for generations. She got out of the car and looked around as she stretched, working out the kinks from driving for hours on end. The homestead area, separated by a post and wire fence, lay quiet and still. Her dad's green and yellow tractor sat in the open-sided shed to the right. Angela's heart ached as her gaze turned to her mother's cottage garden. It was small because of their conservative use of water, but her mother had insisted that she wanted something to make the house feel more like a home. A few stubborn weeds protruded from between the orange rocks that bordered the beds. Angela bent down to pull them out and sucked in a breath. Who was going to tend the garden now? Who was going to run the farm? Her dad's kelpies, Josie and Pippa, snuggled up to her face and licked her cheek.

'Hey, girls. You miss them too, don't you?' Angela said through a sob. The screen door slammed, the sound sharp and sudden. Angela cleared her throat and wiped her eyes, leaving a damp smudge on her sleeve. It was time to step up and face reality.

Charlotte had tossed and turned all night, plagued by restless dreams. Kane had tried to comfort her, but she'd shrugged him off and lay in bed, alternating between crying and half-dozing as her mind fought with denial, anger, and bargaining. Her parents couldn't be dead. How could they leave her? Maybe the police got it wrong. She'd woken bleary-eyed but stayed in bed until Kane drove her over to Ridgeview at lunchtime. She'd looked out the window a dozen times for signs of Angela's arrival. When she finally saw the dust cloud billowing behind Angela's little blue hatchback, she raced out the front door.

'You're here,' Charlotte said, pulling her up into a tight hug. A wave of relief washed over her. Her sister was here. The only family she had. Charlotte's shoulders trembled as she sobbed. 'They're gone. How can they be gone?' They stood together as Charlotte poured out her grief, her voice cracking, her shoulders slumping. When they parted, Angela offered Charlotte a small, sad smile, her eyes glistening with unshed tears. Kane came down off the verandah and hugged Angela, then put his arm around Charlotte's shoulders. Grateful for his strength, she nuzzled into his chest, breathing in the familiar woody scent of his cologne and feeling the steady beat of his heart.

'Let's go inside, hey? I'll make us all a cuppa,' he said. Charlotte let him guide her up the stairs and into the house. She looked back and saw Angela pause, gazing out into the paddocks that surrounded the homestead.

The familiar wallpaper and creaking floorboards were all in place, yet the house felt different, like something was missing. It was as if the soul of the home had been sucked out of it. Kane placed a cup in front of each of them as they sat at the dining table. Charlotte wrapped her hands around the mug and stared at the milky contents. There was so much she wanted to say. Had Angela had the same thoughts as her, been through the same denials and bargaining that she'd been through?

Angela broke the heavy silence with a sigh.

'How did it happen?' she asked. Charlotte's lip quivered, and Kane put a hand on top of hers. She glanced up at him and shook her head slightly, blinking back tears, then dropped her gaze back down to the table. She wasn't sure if she could form the words to tell her sister the details of their parents' last moments. It had been hard enough telling her they were gone. Kane squeezed her hand gently.

'The cops think they hit a roo,' Kane said. 'It was an accident, but damned if it's not a bloody tragedy. Jack and Susan were top people. Real salt of the earth. They'd do anything for anyone. It's always the best ones who get taken too soon.' Charlotte couldn't hold back her tears any longer. Hearing Kane say those words reinforced the enormous void she now felt inside. His muscular arms enveloped her, and she melted into them, feeling despondent but safe and protected.

Kit burst in through the back door with a flurry of colour and jangling jewellery. She marched over to Angela and sat in the chair next to her before pulling her into a hug, then holding her at arm's length. With a nod in Kane and Charlotte's direction, she whispered to Angela, 'Let's go for a walk.' Angela followed her outside. They walked without thinking to the dam and sat at the end of the jetty. As soon as Angela looked at Kit's face, she burst into tears. She'd tried to be strong in front of Charlotte. She was the older sister, after all. She closed her eyes and melted into Kit's shoulder, sobbing and mumbling incoherently.

'I know, hun. I know,' Kit said, rubbing Angela's back. When her breathing had returned to its normal pace, Angela sat, legs crossed, hands folded in her lap, looking at the water. They stayed like that for a long while, staring at the ripples made by the rocks they threw in. 'I know it's not the same, but I was absolutely devo when I lost my mum. We knew it was coming though. I don't know whether that's easier or harder. When you've got months to say goodbye, you grieve that whole time, and then when they finally pass on, the grief hits you all over again.' Kit's mum, Kate, had been ill with cancer when Angela had first moved to Perth. She'd passed away the following year. Angela had come back to the Ridge for the funeral and to be there for Kit. Now, it was Kit's turn to help her through the turmoil of losing a parent. It was a full-circle moment that neither of them wished was happening.

'I loved your mum, too. I think you're right about losing someone instantly. The grief hit me like a truck, but I don't think knowing it was coming would have made it any easier.' Kit put a hand on her knee.

'There aren't many silver linings in a tragedy like this, and it's probably selfish of me to say it, but I'm glad you're back. Even if it is only until things are sorted out.' Angela hadn't given any thought to how long she'd stay in the Ridge. Right now, all she wanted to do was get through this day and then the next. One day at a time. 'I reckon sometimes the hardest battles are the ones closest to home, but they're also the ones that often lead us to the best parts of our lives.'

Angela tilted her head and raised her eyebrows. 'Since when did you get all profound?'

'It comes with getting older, I guess,' Kit said with a grin. Their laughter bounced off the water and gradually faded, replaced by a comfortable silence and a warm sense of connection, as they quietly contemplated life's mysteries.

Chapter 2

Angela and Charlotte stood to the side of the room at the football club and accepted condolences as people left their parents' wake. It had been an emotionally draining day, and both women wanted nothing more than to go home and rest, but they soldiered on. The days leading up to the funeral had been busy, leaving Angela with little time to think. The police investigation was straightforward. They'd found the kangaroo's body metres from the ute Angela's dad had been driving. The ute was a write-off, but the police had managed to find Jack's mobile phone and Susan's handbag, among a few other personal possessions. Angela had contacted her relatives and friends of the family, and she'd put a notice in the local newsletter that served as a newspaper. Not that she needed to because word travelled fast in Sanderson Ridge. She'd fielded calls and visits from so many friends, relatives, and neighbours that the dining table could barely hold all the flower bouquets, and the refrigerator and freezer were overflowing with home-cooked meals. Charlotte and Kane had been having their evening meals at Ridgeview, but it didn't stop the loneliness and silence that swept into the house once they'd left.

The funeral had been scheduled almost a week to the day after the accident. Angela thought it was the biggest Sanderson Ridge had ever seen. The church service had been emotional, and she'd had to stop twice while giving the eulogy to collect herself. But the wake was as lively and cheerful as a rodeo. Everyone seemed to have a story to tell about Jack and Susan. They'd both lived in the area all their lives. They were an integral part of the community, and the townspeople wanted Angela and Charlotte to know how much their parents had meant to them.

Kit handed Angela and Charlotte each a cup of tea.

'Looks like things are wrapping up. I'll stay and give you a hand to clean up,' Kit said, surveying the room. *Not long to go. Hold it together*, Angela thought as she sipped her tea. Tom, Kit's dad, weaved his way through the lingering crowd and gave them both a hug.

'How are you?' he asked. Charlotte shrugged, eyes red-rimmed and glassy.

'It's been hard, but we're doing alright,' Angela said. 'Mum and Dad would have loved that story you told about when you all caught us trying to catch the bus to Perth when we were ten.'

Tom laughed. 'Yeah. You and Kit have been a handful since the day you met. Speaking of handfuls, I'll come around tomorrow arvo to help with the sheep rotation.' Since she'd arrived back home, she'd been so focused on getting herself and Charlotte through the funeral that she had been doing the bare minimum to keep the farm running. She'd fed the animals and topped up their water, but she hadn't put much thought into what else needed to be done. Running a sheep station was an enormous task, and she was going to need all the help she could get.

Standing in the football club with a bottle in one hand, Nate straightened his shirt with the other, then flicked his blonde fringe off his face. Jack and Susan Martin had been Nate's neighbours since he'd moved to Sanderson Ridge a few years ago, and he'd spent a lot of time at Ridgeview Station. Jack was a man of few words, but he was always willing to lend a hand, and with Nate being on his own, Jack had many occasions to help him. There was never any question of whether or not he'd attend their funeral. He needed to pay his respects.

Nate clocked eyes on Charlotte standing with a woman he assumed was her older sister, who had been living in Perth the whole time he'd been in Sanderson Ridge. He'd never seen her in person, but he recognised her from the photos that lined the walls of Jack and Susan's home. He'd been standing off to the side, waiting for the right time to approach the two women and offer his condolences, but there would never be a right time. He just had to get on with it. He took a deep breath and walked over, standing awkwardly in front of them like he was on display.

'Sorry for your loss. Jack and Susan were both absolute legends. I can't believe they're gone,' Nate said, then cleared the tickle in his throat.

'Thank you. We feel the same way,' Charlotte said with a quick smile. Angela followed suit, and Nate turned and offered her his hand.

'I didn't introduce myself. I'm Nathanial Baker, Nate. I bought Fonty Downs from Patrick and Gayle when they moved to Geraldton a few years ago.' Angela's firm handshake had enough gusto to tell him she could hold her own. He let go and ran his fingers through his hair to flick his fringe off his tanned face. There was something about her blue eyes and the smattering of freckles on her face that unnerved him.

'Nice to meet you,' she said.

'If you need a hand with anything, give me a holler. My number's on your fridge.' She nodded at him, and he felt himself staring at her. He saw Kane approaching in his peripheral vision, and he took a swig of beer while he made his way over.

'Nate. Just the man I wanted to see,' Kane said, slapping him on the back.

'Same here. I've got an idea I want to run past you,' Nate said. Kane's connections as the owner of the general store made him the best person to see about buying some new machinery. Kane tilted his head toward the exit. Nate nodded at the two women, then followed Kane, glancing back once before he went out the door.

Kane stood at the railing of the mezzanine overlooking the oval. Nate turned and faced the interior of the club. The din travelled out to them. It wasn't surprising, given the fact that most of the townspeople were in there.

'So, what did you want to see me about?' Nate asked.

Kane grinned. 'Nothing. You just looked like you were struggling with Lottie and Ang.'

Nate chuckled. 'Yeah. Not the best of circumstances to meet someone new.' Kane raised an eyebrow. 'Don't give me that. You know what I mean.'

'Ah, I'm only joking.'

'So, do you reckon you'd be able to get a good deal on a combine harvester?' Nate asked.

Kane's mouth twisted to one side. 'I'm meeting one of the reps next week. I'll see what I can do.'

'Thanks, mate.' They clinked bottles, and both looked out at the oval. That was what Nate loved about the Ridge. Everyone helped everyone out without wanting something in return.

After feeling like she'd been walking in a daze since she'd heard the news about her parents, Charlotte started to sense a new normal creep in. She and Kane had plenty of work to do running the general store. Life went on, and while working helped her to process everything that had happened, she knew there were still so many loose ends to tie up. Charlotte and Kane had left their assistant, John, in charge of the shop and had only been at Ridgeview for ten minutes before there was a knock on the door. Charlotte glanced up as Angela led their parents' lawyer, Samuel Goldstein, through the doorway. Laying his briefcase on the coffee table, he pulled out the paperwork and straightened it in his lap.

'Thank you for seeing me. Once again, I'm sorry for your loss. Are you ready to discuss these?' He held up their parents' wills, and both women nodded. 'It's quite straightforward. Since both of your parents are deceased, all property and possessions are to be distributed evenly between the two of you. However, they have named you, Angela, as the executor.' The terms were exactly as Charlotte had thought they would be. Her parents had always displayed fairness to her and her sister.

'Of course, I must also inform you that any outstanding debts will need to come out of the estate as well,' Samuel said. 'If there is anything else, I'm only a phone call away.' He placed his business card on top of the wills. Angela stood and showed him out.

Charlotte turned to Kane. 'I want to keep the station. It'll always be home for me. I couldn't even think of selling it. What if Angela wants to sell up and move back to Perth?

She's got a life down there. We definitely can't afford to buy her out, not with the loan.'

'That's between you and her, babe. But you've got equal shares, so you'll need to agree on what happens to everything. I'm sure she'll want to keep Ridgeview as well,' Kane said. Charlotte nodded. Kane was right. Ridgeview was their home. Surely Angela wouldn't want to sell it. They fell silent as Angela came back into the room and sat across from them. Kane sat back with his hands clasped in his lap. He looked from Charlotte to Angela.

'Well, tell her,' he said. Charlotte glared at him.

'Tell me what?' Angela asked. Charlotte shifted so that she faced Angela straight on. Her shoulders were rigid, her jaw clenched tight, but she pressed on. Now was as good a time as any to get this conversation out of the way.

'I want to keep the station. Kane and I can help out. I know we've got the shop to run, but I can't even bear to think of selling Ridgeview right now,' Charlotte said, her lip quivering slightly. Angela closed her eyes and shook her head. Charlotte wrung her hands, her palms sweating. Did she want to sell the farm? Was she going to sell everything and move back to Perth? Was she going to leave her again? Angela opened her eyes and looked out the window. Charlotte held her breath and waited for the answers to her unasked questions.

'We're not selling our home. I wouldn't have a clue about how to run a sheep farm, and I certainly can't do it on my own, but we'll just have to work something out.' Charlotte let out her breath. Ridgeview Station was staying in the family, at least for now.

Angela looked in the fridge and screwed up her nose at the paltry offerings. The home-cooked meals that mourners had left had been eaten long ago, and after a morning catching up on farm work, she wanted something greasy and filling for lunch. Grabbing her car keys, she drove into town. A lot had changed since she'd first left Sanderson Ridge. Bucking the trend of many small towns, the population had grown to 1200. The old sandstone pub was still in operation, but the council chambers were newly built, and a house on the main street had been turned into a bakery. The small school had added a third classroom, and next to it stood a nature playground and a skate park that the community had spent months fundraising for. It was still a small country town, but it was far more vibrant than the sleepy little settlement she'd left twelve years ago.

She pulled up outside the general store that Kane and Charlotte had bought a year ago. The shop stocked pantry staples and whatever fresh produce they could gather, but Kane had also expanded the farm supply side of the business. They'd purchased the vacant block next door to house the fence posts, wire, and all manner of small tools and machinery. The bell over the door jingled as she entered. Charlotte was standing at the counter serving a customer, but waved briefly. Angela grabbed a wire basket and made her way over to the shelves. At least this part of the shop hadn't changed. She could still find everything in exactly the same place it had always been. Her phone buzzed with a text.

Just checking in. All okay? Got a date for your return yet? – Kyle.

She'd kept him in the loop during the two weeks she'd been back in the Ridge. He was understanding and said he didn't mind her using all of her annual leave. He'd also offered her unpaid leave. But how long would he continue to be so accommodating? His priority was Mosaic Media and making sure its clients were getting the best service. And Angela was still trying to navigate her situation. She shot him a quick text and sighed. That was a problem for another day.

'That's a big sigh for such a little lady,' a low voice at her side said. She shuddered and looked up as the man moved to stand in front of her. He was dressed head to toe in R M Williams gear that looked like it had never seen a hard day's work. His face was dominated by his enormous mouth, which was currently sporting a tooth-bearing grin. It wasn't a face she was familiar with, but her gut was clenched enough to tell her she should be wary.

'And you are?' Angela asked.

The man took off his hat and bowed slightly. 'Richard Kellerman at your service.' Angela's brows knitted together. She'd learned a long time ago to listen to her instincts, and at the moment, they were practically shouting at her. 'Angela

Martin, I presume. I didn't get a chance to speak to you at the wake. I'm sorry for your loss.' Somehow, he made the commiseration sound insincere. 'I was wondering if I might have a word with you.'

'Me?' Angela lifted a hand to her chest.

'Yes. Perhaps I could visit you at Ridgeview.' Angela didn't know what he wanted, but she knew she didn't want this man anywhere near her home.

'Um...look, I'm not sure what I can help you with, but I'd prefer it if you just let me know what you want.'

He stared at her for a moment. 'How about a drink at the pub then?'

They sat at a table by the window, and Angela glanced around. The Imperial Hotel had been open since the town was gazetted in 1901. It hadn't changed much in the years that had passed since then. The same advertising posters had graced the walls since Angela was a child; there were caps and hats pinned to one wall, and photos of people of every description and in all states of dress were plastered on a board on the other. Richard took a sip of his beer and licked the foam off his lips. Angela sat back in her chair, not touching her drink. Richard nodded at two men who walked past them and said hello to another, and then he focused on her. Angela took a long sip of beer. She'd been in enough boardroom negotiations to know she had to keep her cool, no matter what this guy was going to throw at her. He sat forward with his hands resting around the bottom of his glass.

'You strike me as someone who likes to get straight to the point. Well, here it is. I'm a businessman. I own several properties in the area, and I want to make you an offer on Ridgeview.' Angela chewed the side of her mouth and looked out the window. Tom had mentioned something at the wake about vultures circling, and now she knew what he'd been referring to. Ridgeview Station was one of the largest properties in the area, and with the sheep and machinery, it was worth a lot. Nevertheless, Angela and Charlotte weren't ready to sell. Who knew when they would be? Even if she wanted to sell, she wouldn't sell to this guy, purely on gut feeling alone. She looked him in the eye and swallowed the rest of her beer.

'Thanks for the beer, but we're not interested in selling.' She stood and grabbed her phone off the table.

'Ridgeview could prosper with the right management. Let me know when you change your mind,' Richard said. Angela hid a shiver, then reeled around and stalked out of the pub and back over to the store. Her parents hadn't even been gone for a whole fortnight, and this weasel was already trying to get his hands on their land. How long would it be before someone else approached her with an offer? And how long could she refuse them?

Charlotte was doodling in her notebook, but looked up as the front door was shoved open. Angela's expression was pure fury. Charlotte could almost feel the anger seething out of her as she scanned her groceries.

'What's Richard Kellerman's deal?' Angela asked, tapping her foot a few times before rolling her shoulders back and moving her head side to side. Whatever he'd said had riled her up.

'He's been in the Ridge for about six or seven years. He swooped in and bought that big house on the edge of town. He owns the service station and one of the crop farms about ten k's out of town too. He leases them out. What did he want?' Charlotte asked.

'To buy the station.'

Charlotte's eyebrows shot up, and her mouth dropped open. 'He what?' She closed her mouth into a thin line and shook her head. 'The nerve of some people. He's always given me the ick.'

'We're not selling at the moment anyway,' Angela said. Charlotte nodded but didn't miss her comment. Was keeping the farm only a temporary situation? Did Angela plan to move back to Perth at some point? Angela pulled out her purse to pay for the groceries, but Charlotte waved away the gesture.

'Don't worry about it,' she said. Angela thanked her and left with a quick wave. Charlotte stood staring at the door.

'Did I miss Ang?' Kane said, jolting her out of her daydream. 'Why do you have that look on your face? What happened?' Charlotte rolled her eyes. Kane could read her like a book. It had been that way since they were teenagers.

'Richard Kellerman offered to buy Ridgeview.' Kane pursed his lips. 'And Ang said we aren't selling at the moment.' She waited for Kane to realise what she'd said, and when he didn't, she repeated herself. 'At the moment.'

'Ah. I see. Well, how about we take things day by day for now? We've got enough to worry about with this place,' he said, gesturing towards the shelves. Charlotte knew he was right, but it didn't quell the uneasy feeling that had settled over her.

The wind rushed through Angela's hair, and the smell of clean air filled her nostrils as she chugged along the track on the quad bike following Tom's ute. She was grateful that Kit's dad had offered to help. There was always so much to do on a sheep farm—daily checks on the animals, deworming, shearing, tail docking, lambing, paddock rotation, as well as endless repairs to fences, water and feed systems, and machinery. She had been doing the bare minimum lately, but there were tasks she couldn't put off and tasks that required more than one person.

Josie and Pippa, ears pinned back and mouths open, sprinted alongside the quad bike, easily matching its pace. Angela pulled the quad bike up next to the gate and jumped off to open it. A sharp pang of sadness, like a physical blow, hit her. Opening and closing the gates had always been her job when she was helping her dad. There was no time to dwell on it as Tom called out and told her to head to the far side of the paddock. She chugged her way over to the flock of sheep milling around the water trough and feeder.

Tom's sharp, high-pitched whistle rang out. 'Roundup,' he called to the dogs. Josie and Pippa separated, and each moved around one side of the flock, herding the sheep back the way they'd come. Angela noticed a few stragglers and rounded them up on the quad bike while Tom followed behind in his ute. Once they'd herded that flock into the opposite paddock, Tom, Angela, and the two kelpies repeated the process for the sheep in a paddock closer to the shearing shed. Tom walked towards the ewes, and Angela fell into step beside him.

'I reckon we should do a quick check on a few of them to see how they're travelling. I'll take a look at this lot, and you head over to those,' Tom said, pointing to a group standing further away. Inspecting the sheep, Angela found a few that didn't have tags on their ears. How could her dad have missed them? He was usually so meticulous about tagging the sheep. Tom didn't seem too fazed.

'Not to worry. We'll sort it out quick smart.' They spent the next few hours inspecting the sheep, checking they had enough food and water, and ensuring all the fences and gates were in good condition. By the time they headed back to the house, Angela was sweaty and covered head to toe in red dirt and dust.

'Thanks for your help today,' she said, as Tom started his ute.

'Not a problem, Ang. Call me if you need a hand with anything. You've got a lot to handle here on your own.' He was right, but for the moment, all she could think about was having a long, hot shower before Kane and Charlotte came over for dinner.

The sounds of dusk surrounded Angela as she sat on the back deck watching the sun set behind the mountain range in the distance. The galahs were flying in to roost in the gum trees near the dam, screeching as they soared down and landed among the branches. The countryside itself seemed to quieten down for the night. Angela had seen some beautiful sunsets while she was in Perth, but nothing compared to the sunsets in the outback. The oranges, purples, and pinks were enhanced when the skyline opened up to what felt like infinite space. She cracked open a rum and cola and sighed as the dark liquid sailed down her throat. She felt a deep throbbing ache in her muscles. The physical labour of farm work was a far cry from sitting in an air-conditioned office all day. She heard a car pull up, and minutes later, Charlotte and Kane rounded the corner of the house, smiling. Charlotte held a pizza box aloft. Angela sat up as the rich, slightly pungent scent wafted over to her, making her mouth water.

'Where did you get that?' she asked.

'The pub does them now. Has done for ages,' Charlotte said, depositing the box on the table and flopping into a chair. Kane cracked a beer and passed Charlotte a can before settling into the chair next to her. Angela moaned as she took her first bite, the cheese and tangy sauce dripping down her chin. She realised she hadn't stopped all afternoon and was famished. She had almost finished her third slice as Charlotte reached for her second, but stopped mid-movement and turned to pull an envelope from her handbag.

'This came today,' she said, handing it to Angela, who was wiping her hands on a serviette. Angela had received a few letters addressed to the executor in the last few days, so she wasn't worried as she opened it. Scanning the text, her stomach knotted, and she bit her lower lip.

'What is it?' Charlotte asked. Angela opened her mouth, then closed it again. She could barely believe what the letter said. There was no way she'd convince Charlotte of its contents. She handed the letter over and watched as Charlotte's expression mirrored her own.

'This can't be true. There's no way this could happen,' Charlotte said, eyes wide. Angela shrugged.

'What's it say?' Kane asked.

'It's from the bank. They reckon Mum and Dad are behind on their loan and we need to pay them back in the next 30 days or they'll foreclose on us.' Kane's jaw dropped, then he ran his hand over his mouth and along his beard, letting it rest on his chin. Angela sat forward and put her head in her hands, rubbing her forehead. Banks didn't send these types of letters by mistake. Her parents owed this money, and now, as the executor of their estate, she had to figure out what was going on and how she was going to fix it.

The three of them stayed silent for a few minutes before Kane spoke.

'What're you going to do?' he asked Angela.

She raised her hands. 'I don't know. I guess I need to meet with them and find out what's going on. When's the rep up here next?'

'They can do meetings via video now, so they don't come in person that often,' Charlotte said. At least they wouldn't have to wait long to find out what was going on.

Chapter 3

The pre-dawn darkness still clung to the streets, but Charlotte was sitting in the small office by the side of the counter at the general store, fuelled by one coffee and already immersed in the shop's account records. She hardly registered Kane coming in. He placed a plate of Vegemite and toast on the desk and kissed the top of her head.

'Morning, sweetheart,' he said. Charlotte pulled him down to her for a quick kiss. They'd argued in the car on the way home from Ridgeview the night before, and Charlotte knew from past experience that this was Kane's way of apologising. The news about her parents' financial troubles had hit hard. Kane argued that it might not be their fault, but Charlotte knew it was. Guilt had gnawed at her, keeping her awake all night. When she couldn't stand it any longer, she got up and had been poring over the accounts ever since.

'What's the verdict?' Kane asked.

'The dates on the loan paperwork match,' Charlotte said. 'What are we going to do? We have to tell Angela.'

Kane sighed. 'We will. And we'll just have to figure out what else we can do to help. Don't stress.' Charlotte gave him a lopsided smile. It was hard not to worry. This latest news might just be the catalyst that persuades Angela to sell.

Later, Charlotte and Angela were squashed into the small office, staring at the laptop screen. The white-haired, bespectacled bank manager smiled politely and listened patiently as Angela explained the situation, but he didn't offer them any leeway on the payment schedule.

'I'm sorry, Miss Martin. I understand your position. However, this has been an issue for some time. We spoke with your father about it on numerous occasions. I'm afraid the monies will have to be repaid when due.' Charlotte bit her lip as Angela said goodbye and ended the call. Charlotte understood the bank's position but not its lack of compassion.

'You'd think they'd give us a bit of flexibility. We've just lost both our parents, for goodness' sake,' Angela fumed. She ran her hands up and down her face. 'I don't know how Mum and Dad could have got themselves into this situation.' Charlotte looked at the floor and wrung her hands together. Her stomach churned violently, a nauseous feeling rising in her throat. Despite the potential consequences, she had to tell Angela what she knew.

Kane came to stand in the doorway, and she looked up at him, then dropped her gaze to her lap.

'It's our fault,' Charlotte said, keeping her eyes down.

'What do you mean 'your fault'? How could this be your fault?'

'After the wedding, Kane and I didn't quite have enough money to buy the store and the block next door, so we asked Mum and Dad for a loan. They said it was no trouble. If we'd known they couldn't afford it, we wouldn't have asked. I swear.' Charlotte tried to keep her tears at bay while Kane rubbed her back and looked at Angela.

'It's true. I feel terrible, Ang. We didn't know. We've been paying them back every month, but it mustn't have been enough. We didn't realise they'd taken out a loan to help us. We thought they'd given us some of their savings,' Kane said. Charlotte wrung her hands together. The scowl on Angela's face told her she wasn't happy with this new revelation.

'Well, I mean, they got that loan, plus they lost a lot of stock last year because of the worm infestation. A lot of farmers had trouble getting rid of it, and so many lambs died,' Charlotte said. 'I guess what I'm trying to say is yes, they helped us out, but there are other reasons why they might have struggled to pay back that loan.'

Angela sat back and sighed. Charlotte's stomach churned too much to even think of drinking the coffee in her hand.

'Geez, it just feels like one blow after another. I mean, what the heck is going to be thrown at me next? First, my boyfriend dumps me, then Mum and Dad die on me. Kyle wants to know when I'm going back to Perth, and that

Kellerman guy's sniffing around, and now this.' Angela threw her hands in the air, then put them on the table, palms down. A palpable tension hung in the air, and they stayed silent. Was this it? Had Angela already reached breaking point? Charlotte was about to ask when Angela sat up straight.

'Wait a minute. Do you think Richard Kellerman knows about the loan?' She said. Charlotte's hand flew to her mouth.

'I wouldn't put it past him. Businessmen like him have friends in high places,' Kane said.

Angela scowled and grabbed her keys and phone. 'I'm going home to check in the office. There has to be something in there that can help us.'

'Do you want me to help?' Charlotte asked.

'No. I think you've done enough,' Angela said. As Angela stormed out the door, a heavy cloak of guilt settled on Charlotte's shoulders. Her parents had been in financial difficulty, and she was partly to blame. And now Angela was so mad about the loan that she might just sell Ridgeview.

The sun was poking over the horizon, slowly warming the cool morning air. Angela rubbed her hands together, then shoved them in her pockets as she walked toward the shed. Her dad's battered old ute was still parked where he'd left it. The bottom of the door panels were rusty, and the entire car was covered in red dust and mud, but the engine still ran well. It was perfect for getting around the station, especially to the southernmost paddocks where the terrain got rocky as it inched closer to the mountains. It would be easier for Angela to use the old ute, but she couldn't bring herself to open the door, let alone drive it. She climbed onto the quad bike, and as the wind whipped through her hair, her fingers turned red and numb. She made a mental note to find a pair of gloves.

Opening the gate, she greeted the sheep, who bleated at her interruption to their morning. She hopped back on the quad bike while Josie and Pippa rounded the sheep up and herded them towards the double-sided steel feeder. Angela hauled the buckets off the back of the quad and dumped the lupins and oats into the feeder. The water level in the trough was high enough, and it was clean. A wave of relief washed over her when she saw it. Even the thought of putting her hands in the freezing water made her shiver. The sun warmed her face as she stood next to the quad bike, watching the lambs graze. Josie and Pippa trotted over and sat by her feet, keeping a close eye on their flock. Kneeling down, Angela patted them on the head, then stood and stretched, a yawn escaping her lips.

She'd been up late sifting through stacks of paperwork in the office. Her dad was a third-generation farmer; the scent of animals and earth clung to his clothes like a second skin. But he lacked business acumen. He'd rather be out in the paddocks, working with his hands, than stuck inside crunching numbers. Her mother had stepped in to help where she could, but business wasn't her forte either. Angela had spent hours sifting through countless piles and drawers before she finally understood her mother's organising system. She had found the loan paperwork mixed in with a stack of other bills that were past due. Charlotte and Kane's wedding, coupled with a dry spell and the worm infestation that had taken a third of the new flock, had caused her parents to fall behind. Why hadn't they told her what was going on? She could have helped them. And if Charlotte had known about their financial difficulties, Angela was sure she wouldn't have asked for money. Angela had tossed and turned all night. First the bank, and now the overdue bills. Angela felt as if she was trapped in an inescapable box. She needed to make a decision about the station soon, but if she made the wrong one, the consequences would affect other people's lives. She yawned again and started the quad bike, heading back towards the shed with Josie and Pippa sprinting in front. She took a long breath, letting it puff out in a cloud. She was looking forward to a breakfast smoothie.

Angela sat on the settee on the back deck, looking towards the dam, and sighed. Being back on the station, even with the unexpected events that had brought her here and were still troubling her, she felt more at home than she had in years. There was a comforting peace in the familiarity of Ridgeview. In her younger years, she'd hated the quiet, but now, she found it grounding. She finished the last of her smoothie. After her life had been turned upside down, her healthy lifestyle choices had taken a back seat, but now she could focus. It was one thing she had control over.

Her phone rang, and she let out a groan when she saw Kyle's name. He would be annoyed that she'd avoided his calls yesterday, but she was busy keeping the station running. She didn't need to add to her stress by thinking about her life in Perth. She'd managed to push it aside for the past few weeks with surprising ease.

'Angela. Finally. I tried to call yesterday. How are things going?' Kyle said.

'Sorry. I was out of range in the paddocks for most of the day, but things are going okay here.' A white lie, but a necessary one.

'Right. Well, I was calling to check in and to let you know that we're all thinking of you. I hope you don't mind, but I told the CEO of BCG what happened.' Angela froze. 'I know you've got a lot to deal with at the moment. Maybe this isn't the right time for you to move into a new role. But we could come to some other arrangement, at least for the time being, maybe a remote work arrangement.'

'I...I want the job. It's just...'

'You've used up all your remaining leave, and I've given you two weeks' unpaid leave on top of that. Is there any chance you can come back to the city? I'm not sure how much longer I can hold off BCG Corp. They're keen to speak with you about the campaign, and they'd prefer a face-to-face meeting.' Angela screwed her face up. She needed her job, but she needed to be here. She felt as if she was being pulled in opposite directions, like this was a sliding doors moment in her life, and she didn't know which option to take. Her parents weren't supposed to die and leave her in this position. She was only 32. She shouldn't have had to deal with this at her age.

'I'll see what I can do. Can I let you know tomorrow? I just need a bit more time,' she said. Kyle cleared his throat. Angela felt his annoyance from hundreds of kilometres away.

'Ok. But I'll need a definite answer tomorrow. Either you're back in Perth and on board as senior partner, or you're not, and we'll have to take it day by day.' Was he implying that her job at Mosaic was on the line? She'd been with the company for a decade, and he couldn't give her leeway when she lost her parents. Her phone landed with a soft thud on the wooden table, and she closed her eyes.

Summer in the outback meant intense heat shimmering over the landscape, flies swarming around faces, and red dust infiltrating every crevice. The mercury had hit its peak before mid-morning and was set to stay there for the rest of the day. As Nate drove towards town, the sun warmed him through the windscreen, accompanied by the rhythmic thump of the tyres on the road. He made the trip a few times a week to get supplies, but today he was on his way to the general store to see Kane. He had called Nate with news about the combine harvester. Nate hoped it was good. He turned up the radio and tapped his foot to the beat. With a gasp, he spun the steering wheel, narrowly missing a couple of sheep that had wandered onto the road. Cursing, he pulled over, then got out and chased the closest one. Catching it between his legs, he checked the tag on its ear. It bore the mark of Ridgeview Station. Nate pulled the ramps down on the back of the trailer, then herded the sheep up into the tray.

Angela's car was in the driveway. That was a good sign. She hadn't left to go back to Perth yet. He went around the side of the house and paused as a scream cut through the morning air. His body tensed as his fight response kicked into action. He was about to run towards the sound when he heard a woman's quiet sobbing. This was obviously a private moment. He turned to go, then remembered the sheep in his trailer. Angela was sitting in the armchair on the deck, wiping her face on her sleeve. He coughed, a rattling sound that made her look up, her face red and tear-stained, and her eyes puffy from crying.

'Hey. Sorry. I heard a scream and thought someone was hurt,' Nate said, flicking his fringe off his face. He shoved his hands in his pockets and tried to keep his expression neutral. Angela stood up and straightened her shirt.

'Nobody's hurt. At least not physically,' she said.

Nate's face softened. 'Right. Sorry for the intrusion. I've got something that belongs to you.' Angela tilted her head. He gestured for her to follow him out the front to his ute and the waiting sheep.

'Are they mine?'

'That's what their tags say.' Angela's brows knitted together. 'I was heading into town and saw them wandering onto the road. I reckon they were with the flock in the paddock that backs onto my place.' Nate watched recognition dawn on Angela's face.

'I was up there earlier. I must have forgotten to shut the gate. My head's all over the place at the moment.'

'That's understandable. I was the same way when I lost my dad a couple of years back.'

'Sorry to hear that,' she said.

'It gets easier,' Nate said, giving her a small smile. She bit her lip, and he looked down at the ground, then moved to the driver's side of the ute. He'd done what he came to do. Now, it was time to give her some space. The look on her face told him she needed it. 'I'll drop them back in the paddock before I go into town.'

'Thanks for doing this. How can I repay you?'

He swatted her words away. 'There's no need for that. This is how we do things around here, hey?' People in Sanderson Ridge would give you the shirt off their backs if they thought someone needed it more than they did. It was about helping without a thought of what might be gained from it. That was the way things were done in the outback.

'How about a cuppa then?' Angela said. A smile crept to the corners of Nate's mouth.

'Yeah. That'd be nice. Thanks.'

Angela brought two fresh cups of coffee onto the deck and handed one to Nate before taking the seat across from him. He took a sip and gazed across the paddocks towards the ridge. He could see the mountain range from his place, but it was more distinct from here. He could make out the jagged edges of the uppermost cliffs, their dark silhouettes stark against the pale blue expanse of sky. He and Jack had ventured into the mountains a few times to look for sheep that had managed to squeeze through gaps in broken fences.

'I miss coming here. Your dad and I used to catch up a fair bit. And geez, your mum was a bloody good cook. I'm on my own, so she invited me for dinner a few times a week.' He looked across at Angela, and her gaze fell to the cup in her hand. He cursed himself for bringing up her parents. The loss was still raw for her. 'I didn't mean to upset you.' She glanced up, and he felt a flutter in his stomach. It was the openness in her eyes. His first impression of her had been that she was reserved, but he could see that she wore her heart on her sleeve.

'Oh, you didn't upset me.' She smiled briefly, and Nate felt himself relax. 'It's lovely to hear someone saying nice things about them.'

Nate took another sip of coffee. 'So, how are you coping with things around here?'

'Well, I can't seem to remember to close gates, but all the animals are still alive, so that's a bonus. I haven't been able to get the tractor started yet though. I think Dad was fixing it last time I spoke with him.'

'I can take a look at it if you like.'

'I don't want to trouble you.'

'No trouble at all.' They took their coffees with them out to the shed. Nate set his cup on the bench along the wall, then lifted the bonnet on the tractor. He found it easier to talk to Angela when his head was deep in the engine bay. While he jiggled everything in sight, he told her that his family had a property in Kellerberrin. His mum had died when he was twenty. His older brother, Max, had bought him out when their dad passed away five years ago. He'd wanted to keep farming but felt like he needed to get away from Kellerberrin, so when Fonty Downs came on the market, he snapped it up.

The spanner hit the ground with a thud, and Nate clicked his tongue. Angela bent down to pick it up. He leant over his outstretched arm and watched her long blonde hair fall over her shoulder. Admiring her long legs in denim shorts, his eyes reached her face, and his cheeks burned when he saw her looking straight at him. She dropped the spanner in his hand, and he kept his eyes down. When he glanced up, Angela was staring at her phone. Moments later, she let out a whoop, then grabbed another spanner and slid on her dad's roller underneath the tractor. Nate heard a few groans and bangs and then saw her emerge and climb up into the cab.

The engine spluttered, then coughed, before finally settling into a steady purr. They both let out a loud cheer that scared Josie and Pippa, who had been watching the activity with nonchalance.

'That's awesome. Thanks heaps,' Angela said, climbing down as Nate closed the bonnet.

'It was a joint effort,' he said, wiping his hands on a rag. She beamed and tilted her head to the side.

'So, I have to go back to Perth for a bit, but when I get back, how about dinner to say thanks? I can't promise it'll be anywhere near as good as Mum's cooking though.' Nate grinned. He wasn't going to pass up the opportunity for a home-cooked meal.

'Sounds like a plan. I can keep an eye on things around here while you're away if you like.'

'That'd be great.' He waved goodbye as he pulled onto the driveway. One little dinner together couldn't hurt. After his last failed relationship, he had no intention of getting into anything new, and he was sure that wasn't on her mind either.

Kane was standing near the entrance gates to the farm supply area next to the general store when Nate pulled up across the road.

'Hey mate, how did you go with that harvester?' Nate asked. Kane sucked in a breath and pulled out a business card with the John Deere rep's name on it. Nate flipped it over and felt the breath knocked out of him when he saw the quote written on the back.

'That was the best he could do,' Kane said, shrugging.

'I need it, but geez, that price is a bit steep. I'll have to get back to you on it.'

Nate drove back to Fonty Downs with less pep than he'd had earlier. He couldn't afford a new combine harvester, but he needed it for the crop. Second-hand harvesters in good condition were as rare as hen's teeth out here. There had to be a way to get the harvester without getting a loan. He just needed to figure out what it was.

The chinking of glasses and the low murmur of the pub patrons provided a background hum as Angela made her way to where Kit and her boyfriend Will stood at the bar. Kit hugged her and then turned to the barmaid, Shirley, and ordered her a beer. Angela mouthed a thanks to the older woman before taking her first sip. It felt like Shirley had been behind the bar for Angela's entire life. Angela turned around and surveyed the pub, waving at a group of people she recognised from school. A few of her parents' friends were sitting at a table by the window, watching her, eyes full of sympathy. She acknowledged them, then turned back to Kit.

'Lottie told me about the bank. Did you find out anything else?' Kit asked. Angela shook her head.

'No. The bank isn't budging. Lottie doesn't want me to sell. I don't really want to either. And Kyle's hassling me about going back to work. I don't know what to do. The one person who I would have asked for advice from isn't here to give it.' Angela took a deep breath, trying to keep her composure as Kit hugged her again.

'If you need a hand with anything, let us know. We're happy to help,' Will said.

'Yeah. We can keep an eye on the place if you have to go back to Perth.'

'I think I have to. I just need to decide what I'm actually going to do. Do I quit my job and try to run Ridgeview? Or do I cut my losses and sell it? Whichever way I go, it amounts to a major change.'

'Well, I kind of like having you around. But it's up to you. We'll support your decision,' Kit said. Angela took another swig of beer. She had come here tonight to forget about her problems, not to keep deliberating about them.

'Enough about that. Tell me about you two. I hear you're planning to move in together,' Angela said. Kit's grin was so wide, it nearly split her face in two.

'Yep. I'm moving into the Kitified house on the edge of the Brody farm. Wish me luck,' Will said.

'You'll love it,' Kit said, nudging him in the side. 'I've got to hit the little girls' room.' Angela followed Kit into the bathroom. Checking herself in the mirror, she jumped when someone came through the door. Angela instantly recognised the two women.

'Angela. Sorry to hear about your mum and dad,' Jamie said, swinging her brunette hair over her shoulder. Samantha offered her condolences, too. 'Are you planning on staying in town for a while? I heard you've got some sort of marketing job in Perth.' There was a hint of something in the lilt of Jamie's voice—jealousy perhaps.

'I'm not sure yet,' Angela replied. It was nobody's business what she was or wasn't doing, especially not Jamie and her little clique. Jamie shrugged.

'Ok. Well, I might see you around then,' she said. 'Come on, Sammy. I think I saw Nate come in.'

The toilet flushed, and Kit emerged. 'Jamie's always been up herself, hasn't she? And Sam still follows her around like a lost puppy,' Kit said. Jamie had been in the same year as them, but for reasons they couldn't fathom, had thought she was better than them in some way. It had resulted in her always attempting to one-up them, or, when it was at its worst, starting awful rumours about them. Samantha followed suit when Jamie was around, but when she was on her own, she was friendly. They guessed it was better to be Jamie's friend than her enemy.

'Are they together?' Angela asked.

'Who?'

'Jamie and Nate.'

Kit let out a snort. 'No way. I don't think Nate would go near her. He's too nice for someone like Jamie. Why do you ask?' Kit narrowed her eyes. Angela felt her cheeks warm.

'No reason. Just wondering.' Kit raised her eyebrows, but Angela ignored her. 'Come on. Let's get back before Will thinks we've fallen in.'

On the drive home, Angela pondered her dilemma. She had to give Kyle an answer, but she still hadn't decided what to do. Pulling into the driveway, she looked across at her dad's old ute. She walked to the shed, opened the car door and sat in the driver's seat. The interior smelled like her dad. She looked up through the windscreen and noticed a photo tucked into the visor. It was a picture of her and Charlotte sitting on the back of the quad bike with her dad perched on the rider's seat. As per usual, her mum was behind the camera. Angela looked at the smiling faces. It seemed like a lifetime ago. They were all so happy then. It wasn't only that they were all together; it was the farm. Ridgeview Station was their home. Their own little piece of paradise on Earth. There was no way she could let it slip away.

AUTUMN

"Autumn is the season of change."

Taoist proverb

Chapter 4

Kane kept his eyes glued to the footy game while Charlotte downed her third glass of wine and paced the living room. With a sharp glare, she let out a loud harrumph and then took another sip of her drink.

'Babe, chill. Come watch the game,' Kane said, patting the lounge next to him. Charlotte sucked in a breath. It was alright for him. His family home wasn't at the mercy of someone else. The more Charlotte thought about it, the angrier she got.

'I can't chill. What if Angela decides she can't handle the farm? This stuff with the bank might tip her over the edge.'

'I don't think she's going to sell it. And besides, she can't do that without your permission. If she doesn't want the farm, she'll have to buy you out.' Charlotte collapsed beside him. 'Maybe you should talk to her about it.'

'You're right,' Charlotte said, reaching for her phone.

'How about you wait until tomorrow?' Kane tried to grab the phone off her, but Charlotte pulled it back to her, closing both hands over it.

'No, it's now or never. I've got a few things off my chest, too.' Kane pulled his lips over his teeth and raised his eyebrows. 'There's a lot of stuff I've let slide out of respect for Mum and Dad, but they're not here anymore. Angela needs to know how I really feel about all this.' Kane raised his hands in surrender. He knew how she felt. They'd discussed it many times over the years. He'd told her repeatedly to find a way to move on, but that was easy for him to say.

Charlotte refilled her wineglass and put the bottle under her arm, then walked into the bedroom and shut the door. She took a sip, then a deep breath, and dialled Angela's number. Angela picked up on the second ring.

'Hey, it's late. What's up?'

'A lot.' Charlotte sat on the armchair in the corner of the room. 'I want to keep Ridgeview, and if you don't, then you have to buy me out.'

'Whoa! I never said I wanted to sell.'

'No. But with the bank stuff and your job, and your house, and your life in Perth, you won't stay here.'

'Don't put words in my mouth, Lottie. I haven't said I'm going back to Perth. There's too much to do here at the moment anyway. And this loan has just made things so much worse. Mum and Dad got the loan to help you, not me.' Charlotte's chest tightened, and her breath started coming in short bursts. She knew Angela was mad about the loan, but it hurt to hear her actually say it.

'You left me here, Angela. You moved to Perth and had a life. I had to stay here with Mum and Dad.'

'Nobody made you stay here.'

'I had to. If I left, Mum and Dad wouldn't have had anyone here.'

'So, you're blaming me for your not moving away? Is that it?'

'I'm saying I stayed. I had to do my interior design course online. I didn't get to go to uni and try different jobs and land a fancy gig at a big-shot company. I could have, you know. I'm a good designer, not that I've really had a chance to put my skills to use.'

Angela sighed. 'Lottie, I'm sorry you feel like I left you here with Mum and Dad. I didn't mean for that to happen.' Tears slipped down Charlotte's cheeks, and her breath caught in a sob. 'Do you want me to come over?'

A cry escaped Charlotte's throat. 'No. I'm okay. It's just...' What else could she say? Angela would do what she wanted, and Charlotte had to live with the consequences.

'I won't sell Ridgeview. We'll work something out.'

'Okay,' Charlotte said, her voice almost a whisper. They said goodbye, and Charlotte lay down on the bed. Her head was throbbing and dizzy, but somehow she felt better, lighter. She'd spent years holding in her pent-up anger about Angela moving to Perth. She understood why she'd done it. But if she was honest, she was also frustrated at herself for not having had the courage to do it too. She looked at the photo of her parents on her bedside table. *I'm sorry I used you as an excuse not to do things I was scared to do,* she thought before she dozed off.

The city lights twinkled invitingly in the distance, beckoning Angela forward as her stomach growled, a rumbling reminder of the hunger she'd attempted to ignore for the last two hours. She'd stopped a few times during the trip back to Perth, but she was famished when she pulled into the nearest supermarket and grabbed a frozen lean meal for one.

She stood just inside the front door of her home, taking in the sight of the open-plan kitchen/dining/living room, noticing the comfortable clutter, and feeling the warmth of the carpet under her feet. She was surprised to find that it felt strange to be back there. Her heated meal went down easily and quelled her hunger pangs, but did little to suppress her ruminating thoughts. She still hadn't made a decision about taking the senior partner role or about what to do about Ridgeview.

She dumped her suitcase on her bed and headed for the shower. Afterward, she settled in front of the television to watch her favourite rural romance drama. She knew what drew her to these shows. It wasn't only the scenery or the handsome love interest who was often in positions that showed off his muscly arms and chiselled jaw. It was the relationships between the townspeople and how, for the most part, they were all willing to help each other out. It reminded her of Sanderson Ridge. She picked up her phone and called Kit.

'Hey, just letting you know I made it,' she said.

'Good to hear. Charlotte's here. I'll put you on speaker.' Angela waited a moment before she continued. She hadn't spoken to Charlotte since their last phone call. It hadn't ended badly, but she felt like there was still tension between them. She heard Charlotte call out a greeting. In that instant, a wave of understanding washed over her, the pieces of the puzzle suddenly falling into place.

'I think I've made a decision.' Kit and Charlotte sucked in their breath. Neither dared to speak. 'I'm coming back to the Ridge for good.' Kit and Charlotte burst into a cheer so loud that Angela had to pull the phone away from her ear or risk damage to her hearing.

'OMG. I am so bloody glad to hear you say that,' Kit said.

'Me too! And you know Kane and I will do whatever we can to help out. We'll call in some of the tabs we've let people run up, so we'll have a bit of cash for the loan. It's not all of it, but we're working on it.' Angela could hear the worry in Charlotte's voice, and it dampened her excitement. She had decided to go back to Sanderson Ridge, but that didn't solve the problem of her parents' leftover debts.

'It's all good, Lottie. We'll figure it out. I'll see if I can speak to someone else at the bank. Maybe if we give them what we've got, they'll give us some more time to come up with the rest.'

'Fingers crossed,' Charlotte said. Angela said goodbye and let the phone fall into her lap. Her shoulders dropped from her ears, releasing the tension she'd been holding, and a deep breath filled her lungs and expanded her chest. She felt lighter than she had in weeks. There were still issues to sort out, but she was beginning to feel like she was making decisions that were aligned with the direction her life should take.

The relentlessly cheerful Muzak in the elevator did little to calm the frantic fluttering of butterflies in Angela's stomach. Her jaw felt tight, and her mind repeated the conversations she'd had with herself over and over again as she tried to anticipate how the day was going to play out. The last time she'd spoken with Kyle, she'd told him she was coming back to Perth. He had assumed that she was taking the Senior Partner position, and Angela hadn't corrected him. At that point, she still hadn't decided what she was going to do. Now that she had, she needed to find a way to tell Kyle she was quitting without burning a bridge she'd spent twelve years building. She smiled at the receptionist and accepted the condolences of a few colleagues as she made her way to her office. It felt false to hear words of comfort from acquaintances.

Placing her coffee on the coaster, Angela opened her laptop and checked her emails. Despite her world crumbling, the real world had forged on. Her eyes darted down the screen, and she clicked on a few emails to get the gist of what had happened in her absence. But her sense of belonging to the organisation and investment in its clients and marketing campaigns was gone. Opening a new document, she wrote and rewrote her resignation letter until it conveyed the right amount of praise for the company, appreciation for the opportunities, and hints that she might want a way back in should the need arise. Satisfied, she flung a text to Adam and Lauren, asking them to dinner, then checked the clock.

Kyle was sitting with his feet up on the desk, looking out the window, when Angela knocked on the door. She broadcast a smile, but her hand, holding her resignation letter, trembled.

'Angie, come in. Good to see you,' Kyle said, turning and adjusting his body so that he sat with his hands on the desk in front of him. She took the seat opposite him and cleared the lump in her throat. 'So, ready to get back into the swing of things? BCG Corp knows you're back in Perth, and they want a meeting with you this arvo. I said you'd send the meeting invite ASAP.' Angela opened her mouth to speak, then closed it and bit her lip. Kyle tilted his head, and his brow furrowed. 'You are coming back to Mosaic, right?' Slowly, Angela shook her head and placed the letter on the desk between them. Kyle read it, and his face contorted into an annoyed grimace. Angela felt like a child about to be reprimanded.

'So, that's it then? You're quitting and moving back to the middle of nowhere. You're not even going to take me up on that remote work offer?' Angela couldn't bring herself to speak, so she shook her head. 'Well, I have to say I'm shocked. You've put in the hard yards and are about to be made Senior Partner. This has been your goal for a long time, and now you're going to just walk away from it all. Are you absolutely sure?' She nodded again. Kyle took a moment to look out the window, his expression shifting as he processed this development. 'Ok. Well, we've managed just fine without you for the last few weeks, so given everything that's going on with you, I won't make you work through your notice period. Do you think you can have everything squared off by the end of the day?' He was clearly frustrated with her, and the look in his eyes felt like a dismissal.

'Ah, yep, sure.' She stood up and turned to leave, then pivoted back to face him. Despite his lack of compassion for her decision, Kyle had been a good boss, and she had enjoyed working with him. 'Thank you for everything you've done—taking a chance on me with that internship when I first moved to Perth, then offering me the assistant position. Right from the start, you believed in me.'

'I did. It's such a shame to see someone with your marketing skills and photography talent give it all up to live on a farm in whoop whoop. If you ever come back to Perth, let me know. I might be able to find something for you here.' She spent the rest of the day redistributing her workload to other staff. She wasn't concerned about not having morning tea to celebrate with other staff or even receiving a card from the company. She'd always kept her work and private lives separate, and now that she'd made her decision, all she wanted was to close off this chapter. She'd already contacted a property manager about putting her home on the rental market. She definitely wasn't ready to sell it, but she'd need rental income to help pay the mortgage on it while she figured out what she was doing about Ridgeview Station.

Later that night, Angela settled into a worn wooden chair at the front window of a quaint Italian restaurant, the clatter of dishes providing a gentle background hum to the anticipation coursing through her. It had only been a few weeks since she'd seen Adam, but so much had happened in that time. He and Lauren hadn't made it to Sanderson Ridge for the funeral; she hadn't expected them to. But they'd watched the service online to show their support. Angela knew that in times like these, people always found out who their real friends were. Now, she had to tell them she was moving back to the Ridge for good. She hoped they'd take the news well. She spotted Adam coming through the door. His bleach-blonde, cropped cut was hard to miss, as was the purple and black shirt with flared sleeves. Minutes later, Lauren arrived. They effortlessly resumed their conversation, as if no time had passed at all. Once their food was ordered and drinks were served, the three friends raised their glasses.

'It's so good to have the old gang back together,' Adam said. 'We had some fun times in that poky little share house, didn't we?' They'd lived with each other for four years while Lauren and Adam attended university. Angela's stint at uni was brief, but she continued living in the share house while working. Angela thought back to those times when they were all finding their feet and discovering who they were—their halcyon days. Now they were adults with proper jobs and mortgages, and dealing with things they never thought they'd have to deal with at this age.

'I have news,' Angela announced. Adam sat forward, and Lauren folded her hands on the table in front of her. Angela could only imagine what they were thinking. She soldiered on. 'I've quit my job and I'm moving back to Sanderson Ridge for good.'

Adam sucked in his breath. 'You're kidding?' he said. Angela shook her head. 'I thought you loved your job?'

'I do. I did. But I feel like I need to be in Sanderson Ridge, at least for now,' Angela replied.

'Well, judging by how at ease you seem, I'd say you've made the right decision,' Lauren said.

Now that Angela had started telling people, she'd felt more relaxed than she had in a long time. The debt situation was a problem for another day.

'If that's what you want to do, then go for it,' Adam said. Angela smiled and thanked them both. Why had she even been worried about telling them? Of course, they would accept her decision.

'So, when can we visit? I might see a handsome cowboy out there in the wild, untamed outback.' They all chuckled.

'What about Ryan?' Lauren asked.

'I can look, can't I?' Adam winked.

'I don't know about handsome cowboys, but you guys are more than welcome to visit anytime. And you can bring Ryan with you. Now, onto your lives. Lauren, how's your firm coming along? You've been in it for what, three months now?' Lauren had opened her own law practice after dealing with harassment from males in the last two places she'd worked. She loved not having to answer to someone else and being able to choose the cases she wanted to work on. Adam was happy to keep his job at the architect's office he'd worked at for years. It was close to home, and Ryan's work was only a two-minute walk from his office.

They finished their bowls of spaghetti and gnocchi and sipped the last of their wine before calling it a night. With a final embrace outside the restaurant, the sounds of the city fading into the background, they said their goodbyes and went their own ways. Waiting for a taxi, Angela felt like her emotional cup was full. There was nothing like catching up with old friends to soothe one's soul. And the fact that they'd taken her news so well was a blessing she fully acknowledged. That night, she slept better than she had in weeks, finally sinking into a deep, dreamless slumber.

Shane McGregor's farm was situated about 10 kilometres out of Sanderson Ridge in the opposite direction to Nate's farm, but it was similar—crops in every direction you looked. Lupins, barley, and wheat were the frontrunners. Some farmers attempted to grow canola too, with limited success. Nate tried to stick with the crops that Patrick Fontlass had grown on the land before he'd bought it. He'd been lucky that Patrick had given him a crash course before he handed the farm over. Nate had struggled in the first two years, but he'd got to a point of knowing what needed to be done and when, for the most part anyway. Although on some days, he still felt like he was out of his depth.

Nate rested his weight against the weathered wooden fence railing while waiting for Shane to notice him. Spotting him, Shane waved and stopped the tractor, then made his way through the field. After a firm handshake, Nate made small talk about the weather and the crops before getting down to business.

'Kane got the costings for a new combine harvester. It's way out of my price range even with mates rates. I had an idea that I wanted to run past you. I was wondering if you'd be interested in a shared-use arrangement, like a co-op sort of thing. It's just a thought,' Nate said with a shrug. Nonchalance was the way business was conducted out here. Shane pouted his lips and ran his hand along his mouth, then cupped his chin. Nate let his eyes drift across the crops. This was the first time he'd spoken with anyone about his co-op idea. Sharing the cost of machinery was the only way he was going to afford it, at least for the moment. There were a few farmers on his list, but Shane was at the top. They played footy together and got along well, often catching up at the pub for a beer.

'It might be a good way of doing it. I need to think about it. I'll get back to you in a few days,' Shane said. Nate breathed a sigh of relief. It wasn't a yes, but it wasn't a no. It was a start.

Nate drove back towards Fonty Downs with the windows down and the radio blaring. A calmness washed over him as he looked out at the crops on either side of the road, the sky an expanse of blue with white, puffy clouds dotted here and there. His first official discussion of the co-op had gone well. If Shane McGregor came on board, he was sure he'd be able to persuade the other farmers. His idea provided a solution to a problem that so many farmers in the district faced. He just needed to convince them of that.

Up ahead, the familiar sign for Ridgeview Station waved gently in the breeze. Angela had texted to let him know Charlotte was feeding the dogs and chooks, and Tom was sorting out the sheep, but he wanted to check on the farm anyway. He had told Angela he'd keep an eye on it, and he always kept his word. From his vantage point on the driveway, he spotted Charlotte and a man standing next to a black 4WD. He pulled up next to the car and realised it belonged to Richard Kellerman. Charlotte's face was tight, and her lips were pressed into a thin line; he knew instantly that she was unhappy with the conversation. He marched over, the sound of his boots crunching on the gravel, and stood silently by her side.

'I've told you. We're not selling. Angela's tidying up some loose ends in Perth, and she'll be back in a few days.' Nate stiffened. Angela hadn't mentioned anything to him about coming back, but then again, that was her business. Still, he was glad to hear she'd be coming back to the Ridge. Richard's eyes narrowed before he shot a glare at Nate, then straightened to his full height.

'Well, next time you speak with her, tell her I want a word with her when she gets back. I believe she might be amenable to a deal given your issues with the bank.' Charlotte bristled beside Nate.

'That's none of your business,' Charlotte said through gritted teeth.

'Ah, so it's true,' Richard said. Charlotte was about to move, but Nate stepped forward and crossed his arms.

'I reckon it's time you got going,' he said, the words sharp and clipped, his mouth a firm, unyielding line. Richard shrugged a shoulder and hopped into the 4WD, starting it with a loud rev. He rolled down his window and smirked at Charlotte.

'Don't take this personally. It's just business. This place needs someone with the right knowledge to keep it going and make it thrive,' he said, completely ignoring Nate. They both watched the car tear down the driveway, red dust billowing in the air behind it. Nate turned to Charlotte.

'Are you alright?' he asked and noticed a shiver run through her.

'Yeah. I'm ok. He gives me the creeps though.' Even Nate's stomach had churned when Richard had jeered his parting words. Richard appeared determined to add Ridgeview Station property to his burgeoning land empire, and it seemed like he wouldn't stop until he'd claimed victory.

'I'm glad you were here,' Charlotte said with a small smile.

'Yeah. I just thought I'd run my eyes over the place on my way home.' He wanted to ask what Richard meant about the bank, but he didn't want to pry. Charlotte seemed to read his thoughts.

'We got a letter from the bank. Mum and Dad were behind on a loan. It's my fault. They helped me and Kane out when we bought the shop.' Nate could see that guilt was eating Charlotte up. It wasn't unusual for adult children to borrow money from their parents, especially with the economy the way it was.

'Well, let me know if there's anything I can do,' he said as he headed for his ute. Finding out about the debt must have been a blow to Angela and Charlotte, and having the likes of Richard Kellerman hanging around would be enough to scare some people into submission. Nate decided to talk with Angela when she got back to let her know he would help in any way he could. It was the neighbourly thing to do after all.

Chapter 5

The next few days and nights were a blur of activity as Adam, Ryan, and Lauren helped Angela pack her belongings into boxes and tubs. Angela had used the opportunity to cull some of the items she'd managed to accumulate since she'd moved out of home. She'd been ruthless in her decision-making and kept only practical items or sentimental things she couldn't bear to part with. With each bag of items going to charity, she'd felt a sense of unravelling, as if her belongings had tied her up into a tight ball. She'd arranged with the property manager to put the house up for rent fully furnished. With the tight rental market, the agent had assured her it would be snapped up quickly. It was a relief to know that she wouldn't have to worry about mortgage repayments. Adam had agreed to store a few of her favourite larger items, but she planned to fit as much as she could in her car when she drove back to Sanderson Ridge. They'd spent the previous afternoon amidst a flurry of packing, the air thick with the scent of cardboard and the sounds of laughter as they celebrated the end of the packing and Angela's new beginning with pizza and drinks.

Now, Angela was already two hours into her long drive back to the Ridge. Her stereo picked up a text message from Nate and read it aloud.

Stopped in to check on Ridgeview. All good. Glad to hear you're coming back to stay.

A slow smile, warm and genuine, unfolded across her face. She couldn't deny that she was attracted to Nate. Who wouldn't be? Blonde hair, tanned skin, muscly arms, and eyes as blue as the ocean on a summer day. No wonder he was the most eligible bachelor in the district. The women at the pub had practically fawned over him. Angela cringed at the thought of Jamie leaning over the pool table with her boobs almost popping out. But Nate didn't appear to be interested in the likes of Jamie or Samantha. *I wonder if he's gay,* she thought, then realised that was absurd. She thought back to the day he came over and helped her to fix her dad's tractor; he had definitely looked at her in a way that suggested otherwise. And she'd felt a flutter in her stomach at that look. But her luck in love had been nonexistent lately. She'd thought her relationship with Andy might have gone somewhere, and that had been an epic failure. *No,* she thought, *it's too soon and I've got too much going on to even think about that sort of thing.* The timing was off. She spoke out a quick reply, a grateful "*Thanks! On my way back now,*" and her phone buzzed as the voice control sent the message.

For the next few hours, she alternated between old-school tunes on her favourite playlist and the immersive worlds created by small-town romance audiobooks. She was engrossed in a cosy fireside scene when her phone rang.

'Lottie. What's up?'

'We haven't spoken properly since we had that fight. I don't know about you, but it's been playing on my mind.' Angela didn't want to admit that she'd been so busy sorting out her house that she hadn't given it much thought.

'Yeah. But don't worry about it,' she said.

'I want you to know that I don't blame you for anything. You did what you felt you had to do, and so did I.'

'It's all in the past, and we can't go back and change it. Let's just focus on the future now.'

'Yes. And I'm so glad that future includes keeping Ridgeview Station,' Charlotte said.

'Same here,' Angela agreed. Despite the uncertainty that lay ahead, a sense of lightness washed over her. Tom, Kit's dad, would help her, and, by the sounds of it, Nate would too. If she could just keep Richard Kellerman out of the picture and find a way to make some money quickly, everything would be alright.

In the storeroom, Charlotte stretched her arms up overhead and tilted her body from side to side before bending down and picking up a box of canned food. All morning, their regulars bustled in and out of the shop as they stocked up on groceries and other items. They all knew which days the supply trucks came in, so Charlotte and Kane had been up early to sort and stack stock before opening the shop. With a loud thud and a groan of exertion, Charlotte dumped the box onto the counter. She nodded to the man standing on the other side. Angus Grenville, with cropped white hair as dishevelled as his flannelette shirt and khaki shorts, gave her a clipped nod.

'Mind if I put this on tick?' Angus said as Kane rang up his items. Charlotte gave Kane a sideways glance, sharp and fleeting. Kane stood frozen, unsure of how to word his next request.

'Uh...sorry, mate. We'd prefer payment,' he stammered. Angus's eyes widened, surprise washing over his face, but Charlotte knew this wasn't the moment to hesitate. She took a step closer to Kane.

'We've got suppliers to pay. You know how it is,' Charlotte said, holding a hand up in surrender. 'We're after payment for today's goods as well as any tabs people have rung up.' She pulled out a black lined notebook and ran a finger down the list of names, tapping a few times when she found Angus Grenville's name. 'It looks like you're up to $268. If you can't pay in full today, that's okay, but we'll need the account finalised by the end of the week,' Charlotte said, pointing to the sign she'd printed and stuck next to the register. Angus scanned it, then rummaged in his pocket for his wallet.

'Rightio. I can settle this lot now. I'll have to get Sandra to move some money around before I can pay the rest. I don't like doing that sort of thing on my phone.'

'Yeah, I get it,' Kane said, the corner of his mouth lifting in a small, almost imperceptible smile. 'Thanks for your understanding, mate.' Angus picked up his items and looked at the sign once more before he left. Kane scanned the store, and when he knew it was clear, turned to Charlotte and dropped the f-bomb.

'That was bloody awkward,' he added. 'I hope they don't all go down like that.'

'I know, but it has to be done. We've let it slide for too long, and now look at the mess we're in.'

The bell above the door jingled as the postal clerk came in.

'I'll help with the mail,' Charlotte said. Outside, she lifted her eyes to the sky. Puffy white clouds drifted aimlessly across the brilliant blue vastness, their shadows dancing on the ground below. The sun warmed her back as she moved to the rear of the postal van. A nearby conversation caught her attention; she could hear the murmur of voices, punctuated by the occasional cough.

'Yeah. They want everyone to pay up,' Angus said. Charlotte bristled and turned her head to the side, pretending to search the tags on the postal bags.

'How long have we got? Not everyone can come up with that kind of money in a hurry. If they didn't want to offer people a tab, they shouldn't have started in the first place. That's how things are done in the country. These young ones want to change too much,' said a second man. The voice—a rasping whisper followed by a cough—was instantly recognisable, and a wave of nausea came over Charlotte. Harry Beaumont didn't seem too happy about the news, and he'd give a piece of his mind to anyone who would listen.

'It is what it is. Not much we can do about it,' Angus said. Harry was about to speak, but Charlotte had heard enough. She grabbed one bag and hauled it over her shoulder.

'Gentlemen,' she said in a clipped tone as she marched past them and into the store.

Later, when they'd closed up for the day, she told Kane. There was nothing they could do to soften the blow for their customers. And they both knew how fast gossip travelled in a small town.

After spending the night ruminating on the overheard conversation and going through countless imaginary scenarios in which she handled the situation differently, Charlotte needed a pick-me-up. Leaving Kane to open the store, she headed across the road to the bakery. Beth, the owner, had been in town for about a year. She'd bought one of the small older homes along the main street and gutted it entirely to turn it into a bakery. She hadn't decorated or furnished the interior much, preferring to focus on installing the commercial kitchen and sales counter instead. Charlotte shivered as she opened the door. Warm days meant chilly mornings, but the inside of the bakery was like an oven. She unzipped her jacket, looking around for Beth. The front of the shop was empty, so Charlotte slid behind and called out as she made her way through to the kitchen. Beth jumped, and her hand flew to her chest.

'You scared the life out of me. I didn't hear you come in.'

'Sorry. I'm after a cappuccino, a flat white, and whatever gooey, sweet, delectable thing you have ready to go,' Charlotte replied. Beth jerked her head towards the front counter.

'Come through. I'll sort you out. I've just finished icing some doughnuts.'

Charlotte licked her lips. 'Perfect.' She looked around the shop while Beth made coffee and small talk. Charlotte closed her eyes, inhaled the aroma, and took a blissful first sip of the steaming coffee, a soft moan of satisfaction escaping her lips. Beth's bright, bubbly laugh echoed through the room.

'I feel the same way after my first sip. Mind you, it's a lot earlier than this.' She looked past Charlotte through the front windows. 'Sandra Grenville was in here yesterday afternoon. She said you asked Angus to pay his account in full by the end of the week.' Charlotte's body stiffened, then she let out a long, slow sigh. She knew it was only a matter of time before word got around. But she had to stand her ground. If she and Kane didn't pay that loan, Angela might sell the farm to Richard, and that would feel much worse than dealing with local gossip.

'We did. We're trying to square some things away. That's all.' Beth raised her hands, palms up.

'I get it. If I get wind of any gossip, I'll try to nip it in the bud.' Charlotte thanked her and made her way back to the general store. Sometimes, the weight of everyone knowing everything pressed down like a suffocating blanket of familiarity. With slumped shoulders, she passed the front window of the store and shook her head. The drab exterior had always annoyed her, and her notebooks were full of different layouts and colour schemes for the interior. She stood back on the footpath and sipped her coffee, pondering. If some people thought she and Kane were making too many changes, maybe it was time she did something to really stir things up.

Sunlight streamed through the window as Nate sank into the couch. Lost in the glowing screen's blue light, he navigated the internet's depths, searching for ideas on how to get the co-op up and running. Bizkit, nestled against his leg, let out a tiny, snuffling whimper in his sleep. Nate had been up since 5 am and had already put in a few hours' work. He was enjoying a well-deserved break before heading back out to repair some of the irrigation pipework in the paddock that bordered the Brody farm. His phone buzzed with a text, jolting him out of his scrolling daze.

Ewe can't birth a lamb. Can you help? - Angela

Nate didn't hesitate. He grabbed his keys and headed out the door, only realising halfway to the ute that he'd forgotten his phone and had to run back inside to get it. While the engine warmed up, he rolled his head from side to side to stretch out the sore muscles in his neck. He'd taken a mark at footy training yesterday afternoon and landed badly. It was worth it though. With how well the team was training, it was going to be a good season. They might even win the premiership. He rolled his shoulders back and shoved the ute into gear as his phone rang.

'Hey, Nate. Can you help me?' Angela sounded panicked.

'Morning. Sorry, I should have texted you back. I'm on my way. Be there in five,' he said. Angela breathed a sigh of relief.

'Thank you. I'm in the paddock behind the shed.'

Minutes later, Nate was walking towards her. She was kneeling down, trying to comfort the bleating soon-to-be mother. Nate saw the worry etched in the lines around her eyes, mirroring the concern he was harbouring. He'd never helped an animal give birth before, but there was no way he was going to tell Angela that. Unsure of what to do, he knelt beside her and felt the sheep's protruding stomach. There was definitely a lamb in there, and he had to figure out how to get it out. He moved to the back end of the sheep, and Angela repositioned herself beside him. He lifted the ewe's back leg and could see something, but whether it was a leg, a head, or something else, he had no idea. There was nothing for it. He had to get in there and yank the lamb out.

'If you hold the legs still. I'll try and pull it out,' he said, rolling the sleeves of his checked shirt up to his elbows, then pulling off his watch and shoving it in his pocket. He'd washed his hands before he'd taken a break, so he surmised he was sterile enough. It would have to do at any rate. They didn't have time to muck around. Angela nodded silently, her face drained of colour, eyes wide.

As gently as he could, Nate pushed his hand inside the ewe and felt around. Finding a leg, he grabbed hold and tugged. When it didn't budge, he tried yanking it harder. It took a few attempts, but eventually the sheep let out a loud bleat and, with a rush of fluid, the lamb landed on the grass between them. Angela cried out in relief and let go of the ewe's legs as it tried to twist out of her grip to stand up. Nate used his hands to gently clear mucus from the lamb's nostrils, and Angela laid a hand on its head. Nate placed the lamb on the ground, and the ewe started licking her newborn. Nate and Angela sat back and watched the maternal display with relief and pleasure. The lamb made an attempt to stand, fell, and then tried again. This time, it stood and wobbled to its mother, who nudged it closer to her to nurse.

Nate felt the adrenaline drain from his body, and a grin crept across his face. He'd actually helped to birth a lamb. Angela beamed, and her eyes were shiny with happy tears. She ran to her quad bike and grabbed a rag before handing it to him. He looked down at his shirt and grimaced.

'I reckon we did a good job. It's a real cutie. Thanks for your help once again,' Angela said.

'No worries. I said I'd help anytime, and I meant it,' Nate said, wiping his hands and shirt clean as best he could.

'I think I definitely owe you a dinner now. How about tonight?'

'Sounds good.' Nate grinned, then looked back at the ewe and her baby snuggling together on the damp grass. 'Keep an eye on this one for the next few days. I'd better get back to it. I'll see you later on,' he said. On the drive back to Fonty's, he thought about their plans for the evening. Goosebumps formed on his arms, and they weren't from the breeze coming through the open window.

Flames hissed and crackled, sending a wave of heat toward Angela's face as water spilled over the pot and onto the stovetop. The wooden spoon dropped to the countertop with a thud, and spaghetti sauce splashed onto her shirt. She groaned and turned down the burners, then went to change clothes for the second time. Spaghetti Bolognese was her signature dish, but somehow it was turning into a culinary catastrophe. She checked herself in the bathroom mirror. Smoothing her long blonde hair into a high ponytail, she straightened her shirt and half tucked it into her jeans. A familiar smell wafted into the bathroom, and she crinkled her nose. Barefoot, she jogged back to the kitchen to check the apple crumble that she was sure was burning.

She'd called Charlotte earlier to tell her she had dinner plans, and she was seeing Kit tomorrow, so there was no chance of interruption. Charlotte had grilled her about her mystery guest. Angela eventually caved and let slip that it was Nate. Charlotte had wolf-whistled down the line, leaving Angela cringing. She assured her little sister that there was nothing to it. She was repaying Nate for helping her, and besides, her mum and dad used to have him over for dinner all the time. It wasn't a big deal. So why was she so nervous?

She turned off the oven and was setting the table when Nate knocked on the back door. She beckoned him in and watched as he took off his boots, placing them by the back door just as her dad had done. Her breath hitched momentarily at the sight.

He took off his hat and hung it on the back of a chair. 'Need a hand?' he asked.

'No. I think I've got it. Take a seat. Would you like a beer or a rum and cola?'

'Rum and cola would be nice.' *He's got good taste*, she mused as she grabbed the bottles and poured the drinks, setting a glass on the table in front of him. A sigh escaped his lips after the first sip.

'I can finish setting the table if you like,' he said, picking up the cutlery. Back around the other side of the kitchen bench, Angela served the meal, glancing occasionally at Nate, who seemed so at home in her parents' house. He walked to the sideboard and found the Bluetooth speaker. 'Mind if I put some music on?' Angela shook her head. She placed the bowls on the table as the first bars of a Keith Urban song filled the room.

For a few moments, they were silent as they ate, then they both tried to speak at once. They laughed, and Nate continued.

'Thanks for inviting me to dinner.'

'It was the least I could do.'

'So, you're back for good then?'

'Yeah. I quit my job and rented my house out. There's no going back now.'

Nate raised his eyebrows. 'That was a bold move. Charlotte said you're not selling Ridgeview. She told Richard as much the other day when he was sniffing around.' Angela's body went rigid, fork halfway to her mouth.

'He was here?'

'Yeah. I stopped in to check on things. Luckily, I did. Richard was persistent. Charlotte stood her ground, but I could see she was uncomfortable.' Angela was seething, a furious energy radiating from her like heat. Richard had a lot of nerve coming onto the property, especially when she wasn't there. His bullishness only made her more determined not to have to sell the farm. Astute businessman or not, his tactics were starting to resemble harassment.

'So, you've got a bit of a learning curve ahead of you then,' Nate said, before slurping up a forkful of pasta.

'For sure. Dad tried to teach me the basics, but I was a teenager then. All I could think about was getting out of the Ridge as soon as possible.' She wished she hadn't been so keen to move to Perth, not because of what Charlotte had said, but because she'd missed out on so much time with her parents. She would have given anything to go back in time and listen to her father's instructions on lambing or her mum's cooking lessons disguised as simply helping her out. She could have spent the last twelve years prepping to take over the farm. It was going to happen anyway. Only, it was happening a lot earlier than anyone expected.

'There's heaps of info online nowadays. I'm still watching videos about everything to do with growing crops and fixing irrigation or machinery. I'd be lost without them.'

'I'll definitely look into it. Kit's dad, Tom, has offered to help too. He and Dad used to work on each other's farms all the time. I could also see if there's anyone in town who wants a bit of work in exchange for board. I don't know yet.'

'I'm sure you'll work it out. And I'm next door if you need me.' Angela thanked him. It was comforting to know she had someone close by to call on, but she knew she had to be mindful that he had his own farm to run.

They chatted about the upcoming footy season, and Nate caught Angela up on the newcomers to town. She'd yet to meet Beth, the bakery owner, and one of her old teachers, Mrs Higgins, had set up a Community Resource Centre in the building next to Kane and Charlotte's store.

'Mrs Higgins was such a brilliant teacher. She'll be great running a CRC. It's good to see Sanderson Ridge progressing. When I was a teenager, it felt like I was stuck in a time loop. Nothing ever changed. And Kit and I couldn't do anything without someone reporting it back to our parents. Not that we did anything bad, mind you. But you grew up in a small town, you know what I'm talking about.'

'I reckon the Ridge is a piece of paradise,' Nate said, before finishing his drink. Angela was inclined to agree. Driving back to the Ridge this time, Angela had felt like she was coming home. What would her life have been like if she had stayed in the Ridge? Her little sister wouldn't feel so bitter about her leaving. She might even have married young, like Charlotte did. She could have been a mother by now. It wasn't unusual to have kids at a younger age when you lived in the country. Nate was right though. Sanderson Ridge was a beautiful place to live.

'Yeah, it is. I guess it took me becoming an adult to realise that. Want a refill and some apple crumble?' Angela asked.

'Heck yes,' Nate said with a grin that produced dimples around his mouth and lines near his eyes.

With the meal done and dusted, they moved to the living room, and Angela sat on the lounge while Nate put a couple of logs on the fire. The room was toasty, and Angela stifled a yawn.

'It's getting late. I'd better get going.'

'Sorry.' Angela straightened up. 'I guess I'm still getting used to these early mornings again.' They said goodbye at the back door. Nate offered his help again, and Angela offered to repay him with dinner anytime. She moved to her old bedroom and watched the taillights of his ute as he coasted down the long driveway. The evening had been pleasant. They'd managed to find plenty to talk about, and the silences had been companionable. Angela couldn't deny that she found him attractive, but there was too much to organise for her to worry about any feelings that she might be developing for her neighbour.

The next morning, Kit was sitting at the kitchen table when Angela knocked on the back door of the homestead on the Brody farm and let herself in. Kit and Will lived in a one-bedroom house on the property but often came to the main house. Angela had been in this house so often growing up that it felt like a second home. She would ride the quad over here, and Kit would ride a horse to her place. They had been inseparable. While she doled out muffins, Kit told Angela how she was adjusting to living with a male.

'I didn't realise how many gross habits Will had when I first started dating him. Speaking of dates, how was your dinner with Nate?' Kit said, eyebrows raised.

Angela scoffed. 'It wasn't a date. It was payment for helping me.'

'Yeah, right,' Kit said with a wink. Angela rolled her eyes and warmed her hands around her drink. Winter was definitely on its way. The sun was coming up later and later each day. There had been frost on the grass and a mist over the paddocks that morning.

'Hey, Ang. How's things?' Tom asked as he came in from the verandah. Kit handed him a coffee, and he stood in front of the fireplace.

'All good. I've been doing some research on the best way to get through the rest of the lambing season.'

'Good to hear.' He looked past her out the back door towards the paddocks. His brow furrowed for a second, then smoothed as he said, 'I overheard some of the other blokes talking after church the other day.' Tom had only started attending church when his wife Kate had received her cancer diagnosis. The miracle he prayed for hadn't materialised, but he still attended church every Sunday. Kit had joined him in the beginning, but when it became clear that she was going to lose her mum, she stopped going. Tom glanced at the two women and drew his mouth into a thin line. Angela bit the side of her mouth, waiting for the next piece of bad news to drop. 'Richard's been asking around about your place and the Johnsons. He wants to expand his empire, I guess,' Tom said. Angela gritted her teeth and shook her head.

'What a tosser,' Kit said. Tom's look was a warning. 'Come on, Dad. You have to agree.' Tom raised his hands in surrender.

'I'm not getting involved in Richard's business, but I'll do whatever I can to help you out, Angela.'

'Thanks, Tom.' Angela let out a long sigh. She was an independent young woman, and needing help was a hard pill for her to swallow. For the rest of the visit, Angela alternated between anger and despair. Farming was still a man's game, and she had to find a way to beat the men at their own game.

Chapter 6

The pelting rain caused Charlotte's breath to fog up the front window of the store as she pulled down a flyer and scratched at the old, yellowed tape that had held it in place for years. They'd owned the shop for over a year, but had been so busy learning the ins and outs of running it, they hadn't had time to do anything else. Now that they knew what they were doing, Charlotte thought it was about time for a spruce-up. Angus Grenville's recent comments had spurred her on to stir the pot a little more, but she'd not mentioned that part to Kane. He'd given her the green light to do what she wanted, as long as the customers could find what they were looking for. There was a lot she could do to make the place look fresh without it costing much. She'd made a start on clearing the old for-sale flyers and posters from brands they no longer stocked that had clogged up the entire front windows for goodness knows how long.

She heard truck brakes whoosh as one pulled to a stop in front of the store. Using a rag, she cleared the window to check if it was the supply truck. Kane met her at the door and greeted the driver as he stepped out. Charlotte put on a raincoat and went outside to see if she could help. The driver was already stacking boxes onto a trolley. Kane grabbed the handles, and she held the door open for him. The rain and cold impelled the trio to hurry, and when they were done, they stood at the counter.

'That'll be $1658,' the driver said, pushing the order book across the counter. Charlotte gulped and wrung her hands while Kane checked their banking app on his phone. His face gave nothing away, but Charlotte knew that amount was pushing the limit of what they had left in the business account.

'Alright,' Kane said, checking the payment details. 'I'll send that through now. You should be able to confirm it in a few minutes.' The driver said he'd grab something from the bakery while he waited. If there were any issues, he'd come back in before he moved on to the next town.

Once he was out the door, Charlotte turned to Kane, eyebrows raised and biting her bottom lip. Kane put an arm around her shoulder.

'It's all good, babe. We covered that one. But it means we don't have anything for Ang this week,' Kane said. Charlotte let out a groan, a guttural sound of frustration escaping her lips. Angela had only just decided to stay, and they'd assured her they would pay back some of the loan. Now they'd have to renege on their promise.

'We need to do something. If we can't come up with the money, Angela will sell the farm.'

'I know. We'll sort something out,' Kane said. She wished she had his optimism or at least less apprehension than she was currently entertaining. Charlotte blew out her breath and sulked back to the front window. She ripped off the remaining posters and sticky tape. If she couldn't find a way to make money, she could at least make the store more pleasant to be in.

The football oval was an oversized patch of grass surrounded by bushy shrubs on one side, a brick building that housed the club rooms on the other, and two sets of stands that had seen better days. The spectators not shivering in the stands were sitting in their cars or huddled under umbrellas around the oval perimeter as the rain continued to drizzle. The Merredin Football Club had made the trek to Sanderson Ridge and was losing against the home team. The football was flung in the air, followed by a scrum of arms and legs, with Nate emerging as the victor. He ducked and weaved, dodging the formidable bodies standing in his path, and kicked the ball straight between the goalposts. With a deafening roar, the home crowd erupted. There were five points between the teams, and with under two minutes left, the Sanderson Ridge Raiders played kick-to-kick to pass the time. A high-pitched wail cut through the air as the siren sounded, immediately followed by the roaring of the crowd. Nate fist-pumped Jack Simpson, then felt arms wrap around his shoulders as the rest of the team clambered together to celebrate. Nate checked the scoreboard and donation tally. This game was a fundraiser for their teammate Josh, who'd just been diagnosed with an aggressive brain tumour. They'd raised nearly $10,000. It was more than Nate thought they'd raise, and he was glad he'd been able to help Josh's family.

The chorus of their victory song started up again as they made their way into the changing rooms. Nate noticed Shane McGregor standing back from the crowd. Puffed but still reeling from the win, Nate jogged over to him.

'Ripper of a game, hey?' Nate said.

'Bloody oath. I'm buggered though. I reckon I might be getting too old for this.'

'Nah, you're still a young buck,' Nate said with a laugh. Shane's elbow connected with Nate's ribs, a sharp jab that sent Nate clutching his side in exaggerated pain.

'I've been thinking about your idea. If you can get a few others on board, then I'm in.'

'Alright. I'll see what I can do,' Nate said, stretching his arms up and leaning to one side and then the other.

'Sounds like a plan,' Shane said, slapping him on the back as they joined the rest of the team inside.

The clatter of equipment and the shouts of players slowly faded as the changing room emptied. Most of the team was headed for the pub, but Nate wasn't feeling up to it. His plans for the rest of the afternoon included lighting the fire and watching a movie, or falling asleep to a movie, to be more accurate. He finished dressing and threw his towel into the basket on his way out the door. The corridor was dimly lit, and muffled voices drifted from the office next door. Nate heard Angela's name and froze. He looked around, then bent down, pretending to tie his shoe but leaning closer to the wall.

'Those girls have no right to own a property like that. Angela wouldn't know a ewe from a ram. She's too stubborn to sell it though,' Richard said. Nate's chest grew tight, and his body temperature increased a notch. Richard shouldn't be talking about her like that behind Angela's back. If Angela didn't want to sell him the farm, that was her business.

'She might come around,' a gravelly voice said.

Richard snorted. 'Yeah. She'll come around alright,' he said. A sudden scuffling sound behind him made Nate whirl around. Jack walked towards him, and Nate rose and fell into step beside him. He would have preferred to hear the rest of Richard's conversation, but it would look suspicious to hang around when everyone else was leaving. The two men emerged into the drizzle.

'Nice work today. I spoke with Josh's missus. They are really grateful for the help. Who would've thought we'd raise that much? Richard Kellerman's donation helped a lot. You coming to the pub?' Jack asked. Nate shook his head. There was Richard's name again. That man was everywhere. 'Righto. Catch you round then.' Jack jogged over to his ute.

Nate glanced back at the building, but the blinds in the office window were closed. The door opened, and Richard came out, stopping mid-stride when he noticed Nate standing close by.

'Good game,' he said.

'Yeah. It was. Thanks for your donation, too. It means a lot to Josh and his family.'

Richard waved the comment off. 'It's a damn shame. His poor wife and kids. I lost a brother to cancer a few years back. It's bloody tough on the whole family. I wouldn't wish it on anyone.' Richard cleared his throat. 'Well, I'd better let you go. I'm sure you want to celebrate your win.'

Turning up the heater in his ute, Nate pulled out of the carpark. Cars lined the main street of town, and Nate sighed with relief as he turned onto the road to Fonty Downs. He wasn't in the mood to deal with people. His thoughts turned to Richard. He was trying to get his hands on Angela's farm and might do something dodgy to get it. But he'd also contributed a substantial amount to the team's fundraising goal. Guys like him probably used that as a tax write-off, but there was something in Richard's voice when he'd spoken about his brother's illness that caught Nate off guard.

Nate realised as he pulled up to the house that he'd somehow turned into Ridgeview Station instead. Angela had been on his mind, but he didn't realise how much until he saw her walking towards his ute.

'Hey, what's up?' she asked as he got out. He hadn't planned on telling her about the conversation, but his brain wouldn't cooperate and let him think of another excuse for being there. He stood next to the ute's tray and looked across the paddock towards the ridge. 'Is something wrong?' Angela asked. Nate turned his head and smiled weakly. Was he gossiping by telling her what he'd heard? Did that make him just as bad as Richard? No, he decided. Richard was in the wrong, and Angela had every right to know what he was saying about her.

'All good. I overheard something earlier, and I thought you should know.' Her mouth was set in a thin line. 'Nothing too bad. Richard was mouthing off to someone that he thinks you shouldn't have the farm and that he reckons you'll come around and take him up on his offer.' Nate's eyes followed her face as it contorted from a mask of shock to a furious grimace.

'Yeah, right. I'll never sell to Richard Kellerman. Purely out of principle,' she spat the words and folded her arms.

'Glad to hear it. I just thought you might want to know what the word is around town. I know there's nothing you can do, but I didn't like hearing him say things like that about you.' He made a fist, then relaxed his hand onto the side of the tray.

With a forceful whoosh, Angela puffed out a breath. 'This is why I left Sanderson Ridge in the first place. Everyone is always getting involved in everyone else's business.' Nate let his gaze fall to the ground. Perhaps he shouldn't have said anything. Angela put a hand on his arm. 'I didn't mean you.' They both looked down at her hand, and she pulled it away and took a step back. 'I'm just so sick and tired of people talking about me behind my back.'

Nate shifted his gaze back to the mountain range. 'It is one of the downsides of living in a small town, but I still think the pros outweigh the cons,' he said. Angela stood closer to him. He could feel the warmth of her body beside him as they both gazed at the breathtaking view. She took a deep breath and let it out slowly.

'You're right. Thanks for reminding me,' she said, turning and smiling up at him. 'Hey, didn't you have a game today?' she asked.

'Yeah. We won. And we managed to raise $10,000 for Josh and his family.'

'That's fantastic. I'm sure they appreciate it. Why aren't you at the pub celebrating?'

'Not feeling up to it. I might head back in for dinner later though,' Nate said. Angela shifted from one foot to the other. Should he ask her to dinner, or was it too soon? Where had that thought sprung from? He coughed. 'What about you?'

'Not sure yet.'

'Well, I might see you there,' he said before stepping towards the driver's door.

★

Noughties pop anthems filled Kit's hatchback, each song a reminder of the carefree days spent dancing in their bedrooms, dreaming of leaving Sanderson Ridge behind for the bright lights of the city. Their angst-filled teenage years came flooding back, and they cackled as they reminisced about crushes and awkward dance routines. Now they were in their thirties and heading for a raging night out at the Imperial Hotel. Karaoke night was a big deal in the Ridge, especially when it was the first heat in the biggest competition of the year. Kit had placed second last year, and as she belted out a Katy Perry song, Angela knew she'd be a strong contender again this year.

The line for the bar was three people deep, the music reverberated around the room, and the scent of spilled beer and anticipation hung heavy in the air. Kit lined up while Angela went in search of a spare table. Settling in near the window, Angela scanned the pub. Half of the football team was there, along with the usual barflies, but there was also a much younger crowd, no doubt here to try their luck at the cash prize. Kit deposited their drinks onto the table and scoffed.

'You'll never guess who I just saw,' she said. Angela waited. There was no point in asking who. Kit was already bursting to tell her. 'Nate. He's near the bar, talking with Shane McGregor and Paul Watson.' Angela's cheeks warmed, so she took a sip of her drink. 'Don't try to hide it. I know you're keen on him.'

'I am not,' Angela retorted. Kit tilted her head, and Angela acquiesced. 'Ok. He's cute. So what?' Kit shrugged, but Angela knew that wouldn't be the last she'd hear about it. 'I'm going to order us some hot chips.'

Waiting in line at the counter in the restaurant, Angela let her eyes wander around the room. The décor hadn't changed since the days when her parents would bring her and Charlotte here for dinner once a week. The room was still furnished with the same heavy oak tables and sturdy chairs. Old oil paintings and faded framed photos, some with cracked glass, hung on the wood-panelled walls. A burst of laughter erupted from a corner table where several women sat chatting. Angela recognised them, and her body instantly went rigid. Jamie and Samantha, dressed in tight jeans and even tighter low-cut tops, were sitting across from Stacey and Kylie. All four women turned to stare at Angela, smirks spreading across their faces. Angela felt her face warm. No doubt her cheeks were turning bright red. Relief washed over her as the woman behind the counter called 'next' at the same time as the group dissolved into laughter and muffled chatter. The hairs on the back of Angela's neck stood as she felt their eyes still on her. Stumbling through her order, she gave the server her table number and retreated to the front bar.

'What's up? Your face is all blotchy,' Kit said. Angela finished the last of her drink and slammed the glass down. A few people at nearby tables looked over. Angela glared at them until they looked away. 'Ok. Spill,' Kit ordered.

'It was nothing. Just Jamie and her gang,' Angela said, trying to shake off her frustration. Kit scowled, a deep crease etching itself between her eyes.

'They were nasty in high school, and they haven't changed. I reckon they're just jealous of you with your fabulous life in Perth, and your absolutely flawless skin, and your luscious locks. Ignore them,' she said. Angela clicked her tongue and shook her head. Kit always had her back. If only she could ignore Jamie and the rest of her posse. They had teased her throughout high school for her frizzy hair, her teeth, her pimples—all things she couldn't control. Their relentless bullying had worn her down to the point that she'd contemplated drastic measures to make it stop. She never told her parents, or even Kit, how bad it was.

'I wish it was that easy. I mean, they've probably heard the rumour that Richard's been spreading about me not being up to looking after Ridgeview. Who knows what else that jerk's been saying?'

'You need to let it go. That's Richard's way of doing business, and those girls need to grow up. Come on. Let's dance.' Kit grabbed Angela's hand and dragged her over to the dance floor. The lights were dimmed in this part of the room. The wooden planks that made the dance floor were already sticky, but that didn't stop anyone. Feeling the false bravado that alcohol usually gave her, Angela began to sway and move to the beat. Kit grabbed her hands, and they swung around, laughing and trying not to bump into anyone. When the song ended, Angela pointed back to the table, but

Kit shook her head and stayed on the dance floor. Angela relaxed back into the chair and polished off the last of the chips.

The music died down, and the DJ announced the competition was about to start. Kit had already registered, so she sat at the table and waited for her name to be called. A woman in her late teens in a barely there dress was up first. She belted out a version of *Firework* that was lacking the energy and high notes that made it a banger. The crowd, especially the males, gave her a rousing applause. Up next was a man with long, greying hair and a goatee wearing a Guns N' Roses t-shirt.

Kit leant over so Angela could hear her. 'That's Gazza. He won last year. He's a bloody good singer.' Gazza's version of *Paradise City* got the entire crowd going, and when it ended, the cheering and applause were deafening. 'See what I mean,' Kit said, a worried look etched on her face.

'He's good, but you're better,' Angela said. 'You've got this.' Kit swallowed the last of her drink and made her way to the makeshift stage. The first few bars of *I Want To Dance With Somebody* started, and a few people clapped. Angela watched in amazement as Kit transformed into a diva on stage. She owned the song, and the crowd was right behind her. When she finished, the applause rivalled Gazza's. It was going to be a tough competition.

Someone shouted, and Angela's eyes were drawn to the noise. She saw Nate leaning against the doorframe of the restaurant. His head was bent down towards a woman. Angela could just make out the long blonde hair and tight top. Jamie rose onto her tiptoes, her hair brushing his cheek as she leaned in to speak in Nate's ear. Angela stiffened. There was no need for her to get close like that; the music wasn't overbearing. As Angela watched, she saw Jamie put her hand on Nate's upper arm. He smiled down at her, and she laughed at something he said. They looked cosy. Angela's stomach tightened, and she glanced down at her empty glass. When she looked up, Jamie was gone, and Nate was heading for the bar. She decided she needed a refill.

'Fancy seeing you here,' Nate said when he noticed her standing next to him. She gave him a clipped smile. 'Can I get you something?' he asked. She shook her head. If she spoke now, she'd burst into accusations. 'Is everything alright?'

'It's fine. I'm fine.'

'You seem angry with me. Have I done something wrong?' he asked, his brow furrowed.

She shrugged. 'No. I mean, you're a free man. You can go out with whoever you want.' She saw recognition dawn in his eyes, a flicker of understanding that annoyed her.

'You mean Jamie?' Angela neither confirmed nor denied his comment. He turned to face her. 'There's nothing going on there. Honestly.'

'You looked pretty cosy to me.' Angela hated that she sounded like a spoiled brat. What Nate did was his business. It had nothing to do with her.

'She was just asking about the game.' Nate ordered a beer, then added a rum and cola and handed it to her. Angela opened her mouth to protest, but he pointed toward her table. Kit eyed her from the dance floor, but she mouthed the word 'later' and followed Nate. He took Kit's chair and a swig of beer. Angela looked around but couldn't see Jamie or her friends. She looked back at Nate and met his eyes.

'Sorry,' she mumbled.

He smirked and then sat forward. 'So, why would me talking to Jamie upset you?' Angela sat back in her chair. Why was she upset? Because it was Jamie. Because she actually did like Nate. Because she thought there might be something between them. *No*, she thought. She couldn't go there. The safest option was the easiest.

'Jamie and I have never gotten along, that's all.' He took another sip of beer and then cleared his throat.

'Well, if I'm honest, I don't get a good feeling about her. I learnt a long time ago to trust my gut when it comes to people.' Angela wondered what had happened to make him feel that way. And if his gut told him Jamie wasn't good news, what was it telling him about her?

WINTER

"Winter either bites with its teeth
or lashes with its tail."

Montenegro Proverb

Chapter 7

The scent of paint and turpentine permeated the entire shop, storeroom, and office—a thick, cloying aroma that clung to everything, including Charlotte. She wiped her hands on her oversized overalls and, with paintbrush and tray in hand, strode into the store. Her makeover was starting to take shape. The shop had been closed earlier on Sunday to allow her and Kane to remove the stock, rearrange the shelves, and then put everything back. Charlotte had spent hours researching stock placement and had moved stock around in order to maximise its potential. When she'd mentioned it to Kane, he'd shrugged his shoulders and told her he trusted her judgement. Although his eyes had widened a touch when she'd handed him the paint sample for the accent wall. Still, he had been a great help, and Charlotte was grateful to have a husband who supported her ideas.

She pushed the paintbrush into the tray with gusto and wiped it gently before running it up and down the wall. It was the last one, and she was eager to finish it. She stood back and admired her handiwork, then dipped forward to fix a few runs. Nobody else would probably notice them, but if she knew they were there, they would bug her. She felt a soft smack on her backside and whirled around to find Kane standing behind her, wearing a smirk.

'Oh. Two can play at that game,' she said and held the paintbrush up, aiming for his cheek.

'Don't you dare,' he said, fending her off with a chuckle. 'It looks awesome, babe.'

'Thanks. I just need to get this cleaned up. Then I will have officially finished the mini makeover.' Kane walked to the front of the store and looked around, then walked forward and ducked down a few aisles before emerging in front of Charlotte.

'You've done a bloody good job. I would hug you but...' He indicated her paint-stained clothes and hands.

'Later,' she winked and watched him walk out to the yard where they stored the machinery and outdoor equipment. Taking one last look at the freshly painted wall, she nodded, satisfied, and went into the back to clean up the paintbrushes.

The local newspaper, created and printed by the staff at the Community Resource Centre, slid across the counter. Mrs Higgins cleared her throat to get Charlotte's attention. Charlotte, now paint-free and out of her overalls, turned back to the counter and pulled the bundle towards her, arranging it in a neat pile next to the cash register.

'You might want to take a look sooner rather than later,' Mrs Higgins said. Charlotte grabbed a copy and scanned the front page. It covered the usual type of stories—the footy teams win, a photo of Kit and Gazza after they'd won the karaoke contest, and some advertising for an upcoming cattle sale. 'The letter to the editor,' Mrs Higgins said. Charlotte turned to page three and read the letter, which took up the top third of the page. Her jaw dropped, and then she bit her bottom lip, eventually finishing and raising her eyes to the old woman.

'Who wrote that?' she asked.

Mrs Higgins raised her hands. 'I have no idea. It had been slid under the door before I got to the CRC yesterday. I wasn't sure if I should print it, of course, but we had the space and I have a duty to print the news whether it's pleasant or not.' Mrs Higgins drew herself to her full height, which was barely enough to see over the counter.

'But this isn't news. It's a letter to the editor, and it's downright nasty,' Charlotte said. Mrs Higgins' face remained impassive, and she shrugged a shoulder.

'Angela has a right of reply, and others can write letters of support, but I'll need them by Tuesday if they're to be included in next week's edition.' The old woman turned on her heel and waltzed out the door, leaving Charlotte seething. She hadn't been too fond of Mrs Higgins when she was her teacher, and she liked her even less now. The old woman was probably relishing the chance to create some buzz for the newspaper, which sat relatively untouched on the counter until Charlotte threw it in the bin before Mrs Higgins dropped off the fresh edition.

Charlotte read the letter again. The anonymous writer had implied that Angela had abandoned the town years ago, and Ridgeview Station was now in financial dire straits because of her. It encouraged people to ignore her pleas for help because she "isn't even a local anymore." Charlotte shoved the stack of newspapers across the counter, and it landed at Kane's feet. He bent to pick them up and placed them back on the counter, stopping when he saw the look on Charlotte's face.

'What?'

'You need to read this.' She grabbed a copy and pushed it towards him, open at the letters page. His face clouded as he read the words.

'There's no way we can hide this. Someone will show it to her,' he said.

'I know. Who would write something like that?'

'Richard,' Kane said without hesitating.

'Really? I thought he'd be savvier. Something to do with the sheep or the council. Not a letter in the local newspaper,' Charlotte said, worry etched on her face. Kane ran a hand across his mouth and down his chin.

'I don't know. But we can't do anything about it now. Don't

bring it up unless Ang does. She's got enough to deal with,' Kane said. Charlotte agreed. Angela had only just decided to stay in Sanderson Ridge for good. And they were making amends after Charlotte's drunken rant. They still had so much to do to settle their parents' estate, and with the bank breathing down their necks, this spitefulness was the last thing they needed. Charlotte hoped that somehow Angela wouldn't see the letter, but she knew it was probably futile.

The bank's logo, crisp and official, was inked in the corner of the envelope. Angela's breath hitched as she turned it over. It wasn't going to be good news. With a quick tear, she unfolded the letter, her eyes darting across the lines before handing it to Charlotte.

'They've given us another month,' Charlotte said.

'That's good news,' Kane said. His optimism was starting to irk Angela, or maybe it was just that she was fed up with things not working out.

'Yeah, but unless we come up with some decent money, they'll keep hounding us.' Charlotte dropped the letter onto the counter. Angela grabbed it and threw it in the bin. She paused and reached in, pulling out a bunch of the CRC's newspapers.

'Didn't this only come out today? Why have you chucked it out already?' Charlotte shrugged.

'There's never anything worth reading in there anyway,' Charlotte said. Angela caught a look pass between Charlotte and Kane. She turned the pages, scanning the text, looking for a reason for their subterfuge. She found it on page three. Her name stuck out in a lengthy letter that aimed to spread her personal business around for everyone to read. A wave of heat rose through her, and her fists clenched.

'Who the heck wrote this rubbish?' she demanded. Charlotte and Kane didn't move. Angela scoffed. 'You know what's funny? This part about me abandoning the town sounds familiar. I had someone say that to me only recently.' She shot daggers at Charlotte.

'You think I did it?' Angela shrugged a shoulder, and Charlotte winced. 'I would never do something like that to you.'

'Maybe it wasn't you. Maybe it was one of your friends.'

'You can't be serious,' Charlotte said.

Kane stepped between the two women and held up his hands.

'Alright. That's enough. Charlotte did not send the letter to the paper. We don't know who did it, but my money's on Richard.' Angela let out a long sigh and put her hands up in surrender. Richard wanted the farm badly enough that he probably would try to publicly shame her into submission.

'He's the most obvious choice,' Charlotte said. Angela's face fell. She didn't need this. She was just trying to do the right thing. She said goodbye and headed outside. It was probably best if she lay low until it all blew over.

Pulling into the servo, she waved at Shirley and Mrs Higgins. Their eyebrows rose, but they returned her smile. A wave of insecurity washed over Angela, leaving her shaken. She went inside to pay for her petrol. There was a group of men standing at the counter. She recognised John from the general store, and Angus Grenville and Harry Beaumont, but there were two faces she didn't recognise. They all turned as she walked towards the counter. Angus folded his arms and stood in front of her.

'Is it true that Ridgeview's in trouble?' Angela's mouth opened and closed. 'You're a city girl now. Why don't you just sell it and move on? I'd rather our farms were owned by locals.'

'I am a local. I was born here.' Angus shrugged a shoulder, and John stepped forward.

'Ignore him. He's a cranky old bugger,' he said. Angus huffed and turned back to Harry and the other men. 'It's not true though, is it?'

'I don't really think it's anyone else's business. But I'll tell you, and anyone else who wants to stick their nose in, that I'm not going anywhere.' She pushed past the men, paid for her fuel and stormed out, seething with frustration and anger.

Dark, heavy clouds loomed overhead, threatening to unleash a torrent of rain. The wind whipped hair across Angela's face, and she zipped her jumper against it. She was still reeling from her run-in with the men at the service station. Small towns like Sanderson Ridge sometimes felt suffocating. Despite the wide open spaces, there was nowhere to run. It was easier to be anonymous and fly under the radar in the city. Thunder crackled overhead, and Angela's eyes flew to the ewes and lambs hunkered under the trees. There hadn't been any further issues with lambing, and now the flock was growing rapidly. If she could get the lambs ready to sell, it would help with the debt, but it wouldn't be enough.

Angela moved closer to the rusty windmill that stood like a beacon in the middle of the paddock. It was as old as the house, probably older. The blades whirred faster as the wind picked up. It was definitely time to head inside before the storm started. Angela sat on the quad bike and turned the key. Nothing. She switched it off and checked the fuel level. There was plenty in the tank. She turned the key again, but the engine wouldn't start. Fantastic, she thought. She looked up at the sky.

'What else? What else are you going to throw at me? How much more do you think I can take?' She yelled as tears welled in her eyes. 'Why did you have to die? I need you. Charlotte needs you. We can't do this on our own.' Overwhelmed, she slumped forward, her head resting on her arms draped across the handlebars as the pent-up feelings escaped in a torrent of tears. Raindrops pinged on her back, but she didn't move. 'It's not fair,' she cried. 'I'm trying. I don't know what else to do.' Thunder rumbled overhead, and fat droplets of rain hit her. She sighed and tried the key again. 'Come on. Please.' The engine spluttered to life, and she cried out, relief flooding through her as she rode hard and fast to the safety of the house.

A soft layer of red dust caked Angela's fingertips as she ran them along her mother's dresser. Her parents' bedroom had sat untouched since she'd arrived back home. She shivered and rubbed her hands together. The warmth of the wood fire hadn't reached under the closed door. She took in the perfectly made bed, her mother's bedside table with her reading glasses resting neatly on a book, her father's, the opposite—a mess of papers, a book he'd been reading for a year, cups, and an old clock radio he refused to part with despite having a mobile phone with a perfectly good alarm. A bittersweet smile, tinged with happiness and sorrow, crept across Angela's face. Wrapping her mother's dressing gown around her, she lay down on her mother's side of the bed. The weight of lost time pressed down, each childhood memory a sharp pang, while an uncertain future stretched before her. Her parents would never see her get married. They'd never see their grandchildren. They'd never grow old together. The farm they'd worked so hard on was in jeopardy, and Angela had let everyone down. Tears fell onto the pillow until her shoulders finally stopped shaking.

★

Nate watched Shane's ute head back down the long, winding driveway. He jolted as the thunder clapped overhead. The storm seemed to come in waves, each one bringing a fresh deluge of rain and howling wind. Shane had visited on the premise of bringing Nate the meat pack he'd won at the pub, but he'd slipped his concerns for the co-op into their conversation. Nate had tried to hide his disappointment, but now he picked up a rock and threw it as far as he could.

He looked up as a ute pulled into his driveway. Another round of rain sheeted down as Angela jumped out of the car and ran to where he now stood on the verandah.

'Geez, I need to work out more,' she said, puffing. Nate laughed at the absurdity of her comment. She was far from unfit. Despite the fluffy jumper she was wearing, he knew her body was toned underneath. Pulling his gaze away from her, he opened the back door and waved her in. Then he headed to the kitchen and made them both a coffee. 'Thanks,' she said as she folded both hands around the cup. The close proximity allowed him to study her face. Her eyes were red-rimmed and slightly puffy. Nate took up prime position in front of the wood fire, and she stood next to him, her shoulders rising and falling in a stretch.

'To what do I owe the pleasure?' he asked. Angela closed her eyes and took another sip of coffee. Her shoulders left her ears, and she sighed and glanced up at him.

'Can't a girl randomly drop by her neighbour's house?'

'Of course. You can visit Fonty Downs anytime.' He caught a blush on her cheeks that mirrored his own. She shifted from one foot to the other.

'I just…I'm struggling.' He leant down to put another log on the fire so that she could continue without scrutiny. 'The bank sent me another letter. Charlotte and Kane are trying to pay the money back, but they still have to run the store. I need to make my final payout from work last until I figure out what I'm doing. I feel like everything's against me. I want to keep Ridgeview, but honestly, I don't know if I can.' Nate stood up, and their hands brushed. A zap of electricity ran through them, but neither of them drew away.

'I can't tell you what to do, but Ridgeview Station is your parents' legacy. It's been in your family for generations. You know, your dad told me that Richard had spoken with him about a partnership. Your dad wouldn't have a bar of it. He said Ridgeview belonged to you and Charlotte. He believed it was going to pass on to you two and then your children, and their children, and so on.' Angela's eyes welled. *Damn it*, he thought. He'd said the wrong thing. It wasn't his place to tell her to stay. She had every right to sell that farm if she wanted to.

'I don't want to sell it, but how can I keep it?' Angela was on the brink of tears, and Nate desperately wanted to wrap his arms around her.

'There's got to be a way,' he said, grabbing paper and a pen from a drawer in the kitchen and beckoning her to the table.

He wrote Ridgeview Station at the top and the number one on the side, then chewed the end of the pen. He looked out the back door for a moment, then bent over the paper again, scribbling for a few minutes. He slid the paper across the table towards Angela; she scanned his hastily scribbled notes, a slow smile blooming.

Nodding, she said, 'Yep. I can sell the lambs when they're ready. And Mum's car is sitting there unused. There's probably other stuff in the house I can sell. I mean, it'll be hard to part with some of it, but if that's what it takes, then I have to do it.' She leant back and looked out the back door towards the crops. Nate could almost see the cogs in her head working. He lapsed into thinking about how nice it was to have her in his house, jolting when she suddenly sat up.

'I have an idea. I don't know exactly how we could do it, but it's more long-term than anything else we've come up with.' Nate's ears clung to the word we, and he felt a flutter in his chest.

'I'm listening,' he said.

'What if I turn part of the land into a farm stay? Station stays are becoming popular, and Sanderson Ridge is great for tourists who like farm and outback vibes.' Nate's eyes widened, and he grinned.

'Bloody hell. That's brilliant.' She beamed, and his heart thumped like a drum. 'I think it'd be the first one out this way. It'll take a fair bit to set up, but I'm sure we can do it.'

She put a hand on his and squeezed gently, then pulled back.

'Thanks, Nate. That means a lot. Do you really think it could work?' It would take time and money. Neither of which she didn't have in abundance, but it would keep her in the Ridge.

'You're a marketing whiz, aren't you? And a talented photographer. You'll make it look so good that everyone will want to visit.' She laughed and grabbed the paper, writing furiously. They spent the next hour brainstorming ideas. As she left, the lightness in her step and the sparkle in her eyes made his heart race with a mixture of relief and something akin to hope.

Chapter 8

Charlotte flipped the sign on the door and opened it to let Beth in. She was holding two coffee cups and handed one to Charlotte, who smiled appreciatively after taking her first sip. Beth surveyed the newly renovated store, eyes wide, taking in the transformation. The store still smelled of fresh paint. The walls were now off-white, which opened up the space, making it light and airy. The shelves had been centred, and the old stock that was a relic from the previous owners had been sold off at a discount or thrown out. What was left was cleaned and stacked neatly onto the shelves in coherent and appropriate sections rather than haphazard arrays. The front window was clear of posters and now displayed a vignette featuring their most popular winter products on a small table and a mannequin wearing a raincoat and gumboots standing under a cloud made of cardboard and cotton balls. Charlotte had plans to change the window display seasonally, if not monthly, hoping that it might turn into a drawcard for the store. The whole makeover had taken a few weeks, and it hadn't cost them anything since they already had the paint and equipment, but it had completely transformed the store and created a fresh and inviting feel. It always amazed Charlotte how much paint and décor could change a person's enjoyment of a space. She'd been lucky that her parents had encouraged her creativity by letting her paint her bedroom and rearrange the furniture. The addition of mirrors, lighting, and a couple of well-placed throw pillows had added to its appeal as a teenager's haven. Her mother had even asked her advice on decorating the living areas in the house.

Beth walked over to the window display, retrieved the fallen umbrella, and placed it back on the table. With a thoughtful frown, she gazed around the store, then settled her eyes back on Charlotte's face.

'I love what you've done with this place. It feels like a brand new shop. Well done!' Charlotte beamed and thanked her. She hadn't done it for the praise, but the warmth of Beth's compliment sent a delightful shiver down her spine. She shrugged a shoulder. 'I didn't do much really. Just a tidy-up and some paint.'

'Well, you might say it's not much, but what you have done has really enhanced the shop. It feels so welcoming now.' Beth straightened her spine and tilted her head. 'How would you like to do the bakery next?' *Heck yes*, Charlotte thought. The bakery boasted delicious food but felt starved of ambience. Beth continued, 'I might be a talented baker, but I'm rubbish at decorating. I'd pay you, of course.' Charlotte would have done it for free, but to be offered money was even better. Her head was already buzzing with a million different ideas. 'Come up with some ideas and costings and we'll go from there,' Beth said.

'Are you serious? That would be great.'

'It's a win-win for us both. Now, I'll just get what I came in for and leave you to it.'

As soon as Beth left, Charlotte ran to find Kane. The storeroom was jam-packed with old furniture and stock that Charlotte hadn't wanted displayed until next season. She moved an old display stand with a missing bottom shelf out of the way.

'Kane. Are you in here?' she called. A dropped tin clanked loudly, followed by a muttered swear word that echoed off the walls. Kane hobbled around some boxes and stood in front of her, bending to rub the top of his foot.

'Geez, you scared me. What's up?' She lifted his arm so that he stood in front of her, and she hugged him, tilting her head to look into his face. She couldn't stop smiling. 'You look like the cat who got the cream. Good news, I take it?'

'Beth just asked me to redesign the bakery. And she's going to pay me.' Kane squeezed her, and she felt her insides bunch.

'That's awesome. I knew your makeover would be a good thing,' he said with a wink. Charlotte playfully jabbed him in the ribs, and he feigned hurt. He hadn't been so keen on her making this many changes to the shop, but once he'd seen the results, he'd called her a genius.

'Well, I'd better get started on some concepts and maybe sketch a few mock-ups.'

'Look at you busting out the fancy lingo. Maybe you should start your own interior design business.'

'Maybe I should,' she said. He'd meant it as a lighthearted joke, but the idea lodged itself firmly in her subconscious.

With a sketchpad in one hand and a pencil in the other, Charlotte was in the zone. She'd spent an hour researching bakery renovations. A few different ideas had stood out, but she'd settled on a theme that she thought Beth would go for. Head down, eyes on the page, she jolted when Angela said 'hey' and plonked herself onto the couch opposite her. They hadn't spoken since the newspaper came out, but Angela seemed to be in much better spirits than she had been that day.

'I've got some good news,' she said.

'Cool. Me too,' Charlotte replied.

'Okay, I'll go first. Nate and I were thinking.' Charlotte smothered a smile. 'Don't give me that look.' Angela threw a cushion at Charlotte. 'Anyway, we were thinking of ways to make Ridgeview financially viable for the future, and we came up with a plan. I'm going to start a farm stay.' Charlotte had to admit it was a great idea. It wouldn't solve their immediate problem, but it would help keep Ridgeview going well into the future.

'That's brilliant. Let me know what Kane and I can do. My news is that Beth asked me to redesign the interior of the bakery.'

'Lottie, that's great news. I was actually going to ask you to help with decorating the farm stay.'

'I can do both.'

'Awesome. I need to pay back that loan before anything else though. I'm going to sell the lambs and a few other things. Like mum's car.' Charlotte froze. They hadn't discussed what they'd do with their parents' belongings. 'I know it's going to be hard. But we can do it together. We have to if we want to keep Ridgeview.'

It felt like they'd only just passed away, but her parents had been gone for over a month. Was she ready to sort through their personal belongings? It felt like she was losing her last link to them.

Angela watched from the safety of the sparsely furnished terminal lounge as the plane landed on the runway with a thud. It had been weeks since their dinner date, but in a few brief moments, she'd see Adam and Lauren again. She never thought they'd take her up on her offer to visit, but she was looking forward to showing them her hometown. When she'd finally confessed about the debt and told them her solution, they'd booked flights and a few days off work. They'd never been this far north of Perth before. Lauren was more suited to the courtroom, and Adam had grown accustomed to air-conditioned offices overlooking the Swan River. She watched them exit the plane and saw their faces blanch slightly at the size of the terminal. After a loud, lingering greeting, they refuelled the car with petrol and themselves with food and were ready to tackle the rest of the drive to Sanderson Ridge.

By the time they'd pulled up at Ridgeview Station, Adam had filled her in on his latest news—he and Ryan had moved in together and were getting a puppy. It was a huge step for him. And Lauren had recently landed a big case, but couldn't go into details in case it jeopardised the lawsuit. Angela had admitted how hard things had been, but now that she had their support, she felt a lightness overcome her. She gave them a quick tour of the house and, over dinner, told them about Nate.

'He's just a friend,' Angela said.

'Mmm hmm. And I'm the Prime Minister,' Adam replied, with a knowing look. Lauren burst out laughing.

'He sounds like a great guy to have around. Will he help you get the farm stay up and running?' she asked.

'He said he would help with whatever I needed. I'll introduce you to him tomorrow. And to Charlotte and Kane, and we'll probably see Kit as well.' It had been a long day for all of them. Angela fell asleep quicker and easier than she had in weeks. She hadn't realised how lonely the empty house had felt until people were in it.

Angela, Adam, and Lauren sat in the ute behind Nate's and watched him open the gate, then jumped back into his ute.

'You weren't joking when you said he was cute,' Adam said. Angela and Lauren rolled their eyes. 'What? A hot guy is a hot guy, straight or otherwise.'

'He's clearly taken,' Lauren said. Angela glared at her. 'If you can't tell he's keen on you, you're blind.'

'Shhhh,' Angela whispered as Nate approached the ute. They climbed out and all stood together looking across the paddock. The homestead and large shed were in the distance to their right, and the rocky outcrops of Sanderson Ridge loomed large but far off to their left. It was the perfect spot for the accommodation.

'So, what are you thinking? A tiny home type of thing?' Adam asked.

'Yeah, I think so. Maybe we could have a few options. You know, one for a couple, another for a family.'

'Hold up. Have you run this by the shire yet?' Lauren asked. Angela shook her head. 'That's okay. I can help with that side of things. And you'll need to get the business up and running—insurances, registrations.' Angela felt a pang of trepidation. Now it was becoming real. Nate and Adam started walking towards the mountains, their voices drifting back to where Angela and Lauren stood.

'They're getting along well,' Angela said.

'Of course. Adam gets along with everyone.' While they waited for Nate and Adam, they went over the legalities of the farm stay. It was daunting, but Angela felt buoyed by the fact that she had the right people helping her.

Nate watched Adam get in the passenger seat next to Angela for the drive back to the homestead. They were clearly close, but how close? Had they dated? Did they have feelings for each other? And why was it worrying him? He shrugged off his concerns and shifted the ute into gear.

'Do you want to come in for a drink?' Angela asked when Nate pulled up near the shed and joined them. He wanted to stay, but knew Angela probably wanted to hang out with her friends.

'Nah, I'd better get back to it. I've got a bit to do before the next cold front hits,' Nate said.

'Mind if I tag along?' Adam asked. Nate jerked his head towards the other man. 'It's okay if you've got something on. I just thought I'd give these two a chance to get into the nitty-gritty of the legal stuff, and that's not my forte,' Adam said, his hands up in surrender. It would be awkward having Adam at his place, but Nate felt like he didn't have a choice. Angela was watching his reaction.

'Right. Yeah, okay then. I mean, I can show you around Fonty Downs and maybe drive into town later on.' He turned to Angela. 'How about you two meet us for lunch at the bakery?'

Nerves kept his lips sealed as he drove the short distance back to his farm. Adam talked enough for the two of them. When Nate pulled up in the carport, he already knew that they'd all shared a house in their early teens, that Adam had been working at a new architecture firm for a few months, and that he'd recently moved in with his boyfriend, Ryan. Nate had almost choked when that information was revealed. His theory about Adam being the reason Angela was so hot and cold had been blown apart.

'What? You didn't realise I was gay?' Nate shut the car door and pulled his hat down, avoiding Adam's eyes.

'Well, honestly, no. I mean, you're not flamboyant or anything. You're a regular bloke.'

'Most of us are,' Adam shot back. Nate raised a hand in apology and bent down to pat his kelpie, Bizkit. He introduced him to Adam.

'Bizkit?' Adam queried. Nate chuckled.

'Yeah. As in Limp Bizkit.' Adam made the sign of the horns, the universal hand gesture for rock and metal music, with his right hand. Adam was full of surprises, and Nate cursed himself again for making assumptions.

They fell into step as they walked towards the grain silos that sat close to the shed. He explained the farm in terms that he hoped made him sound intelligent. Adam seemed interested and asked Nate about how he came to be in the Ridge. Nate gave him the quick version and then shifted the conversation to Angela's plan.

'You reckon you can design something good on the cheap?' Nate asked.

'I'll try. Whatever material we use has to be easily transported out here to the middle of nowhere. So it'll have to be something light and, hopefully, that means cheap,' Adam said. Light and cheap. Nate's mind ticked over. Not bricks, then. Maybe wood and plasterboard. His eyes darted across to the old silo lying on its side.

'What about that?' he said, pointing to it. Adam's eyes followed Nate's hand, and his face lit up.

'That's brilliant. I'll make it work, and it'll be a unique selling point for marketing. "Come and stay at a working sheep station and sleep in a silo".' They walked over and inspected it. Despite sitting unused, it was largely free of rust, and the sides only had a couple of minor dents, which added to the authenticity and charm. Nate ran inside and grabbed Adam a pencil and notepad, and watched as he created some rough sketches of what the silo could look like. Nate could picture it in his mind, and he hoped Angela could too.

Lauren looked out of place, dressed in a vintage polka dot dress, with her cropped dark hair (she'd ditched the bleach blonde years ago), and bright red sunglasses that covered half her face. Her appearance drew the eyes of everyone the trio passed as they walked up the road to the bakery. Strangers usually garnered attention, but Angela didn't think someone with Lauren's fashion sense had been in Sanderson Ridge for a long time. *Wait until they see Adam at the pub on Friday night*, she mused.

'Maybe I should have worn jeans,' Lauren said, as Mrs Higgins brushed past them with a scowl on her face.

'Nah. You do you,' Angela replied.

'You sound like Adam.' Angela blew her a kiss and she laughed. She heard a snicker and glanced up to see Jamie and Sam walking towards them.

'I hear you're back for good. Some people in Sanderson Ridge aren't keen on people who move away coming back to take over,' Jamie said. Angela scowled, and Lauren took a step closer to her.

 'It was you, wasn't it?' Angela said.

'I have no idea what you're talking about.'

'I could take you to court for slander.' Lauren looked between the two women.

'I may or may not have written that letter. But you and I both know it was the truth. You moved to Perth. Some of us didn't leave town. What right do you have to come back here, swanning around like you own the place, and nabbing the only eligible bachelor in town?'

Angela's eyes widened in recognition. This had nothing to do with her leaving the Ridge. Jamie must have seen Nate having a drink with Angela after he'd turned her down.

'You did it because of Nate?' Angela asked, incredulous. Jamie pursed her lips and shrugged.

Sam shifted from one foot to the other. 'Let's go. Mackenzie's waiting,' she said. Jamie smirked again and then pushed past Angela and Lauren. Angela closed her eyes and took a deep breath.

'What was all that about?' Lauren asked.

'That was Jamie and Sam. From high school.' Lauren's eyes widened. High school dramas are universal.

'It sounded to me as if she was jealous of you. But if you can prove that she slandered you, I'll win that case in a flash.'

'Thanks, but I've got more important things on my mind.'

Pushing open the bakery door, the acrid smell of fresh paint filled her nostrils, and she fanned a hand in front of her face. She ushered Lauren inside, then propped the door open with a brick to let some fresh air in. Judging by the sounds of rhythmic mixing and banging coming from the kitchen, Beth was busy baking. Charlotte was sitting on the floor putting together a flat-pack coffee table. Angela sat next to her and introduced Lauren, then grabbed an Allen key and got to work on a set of shelving units.

'This place is coming together nicely,' Angela said as she fixed two panels together.

'I've got a lot more to do. But you get what I'm going for, right?' Charlotte's brows knitted together.

'Absolutely. Retro 1950s diner. My kind of place,' Lauren said. Charlotte beamed, her eyes sparkling with delight.

'Need a hand?' Nate said, coming through the door with Adam in tow. Angela's gaze was drawn to Nate's face and the smattering of wrinkles that lined his eyes when he grinned. After introducing Charlotte and Adam, the group ordered food and drinks and settled at the only table that was upright. Their seating consisted of chairs, stools, and overturned milk crates. Beth apologised for the mess when she brought out their orders.

'No worries. This place is going to look fab when Lottie's finished,' Angela said, winking at Charlotte. It was a gesture their dad made when they'd won awards at school, when Charlotte had won colouring-in competitions, or when Angela had won photography competitions. It didn't matter if it was a minor achievement. Jack Martin always made sure his daughters knew he was proud of them. Angela could tell that Charlotte was thinking about it too and looked away to avoid the pain in her little sister's eyes.

'So, we've had an idea. Well, actually it was Nate's brainwave, but we're running with it,' Adam said before shoving some hot chips into his mouth. When Angela shot a glance at Nate, his cheeks bloomed with embarrassed colour. Adam swallowed and continued. 'What if we make the accommodation out of a silo?' Angela's jaw dropped.

'That's a unique idea. I can picture it already. The marketing campaign will be awesome. But how much is a silo going to set us back? We've got a tight budget, remember.'

'I've got an old one lying around that you can have,' Nate said.

'Seriously? Oh, I couldn't,' Angela said, shaking her head.

'You have to, Ang. I've already drawn it up. It's going to be mint. Check this out,' Adam said, passing her the notepad. His sketches were raw, but she could see his vision. A silo would be a drawcard. Instantly, her marketing brain kicked into gear, ideas swirling in her mind. She was already thinking about the photographs she could take and how they would look on a website, postcards, or even a TV commercial. She looked over at Nate.

'Are you sure?'

'Yeah. Of course. But you'll have to get it approved by the shire though.' Angela agreed. She was getting ahead of herself. There were a lot of hurdles to jump before they could even start working on it for real.

'I reckon the shire will go for it,' Charlotte said. Everyone nodded. 'Well, I'd better get back to it. Nice meeting you two.'

Nate finished his drink and cleared his throat. 'Lauren, can I pick your brain about something?' Lauren raised her eyebrows, then agreed. Nate launched into a speech he'd obviously rehearsed prior. Angela's stomach churned as she listened. Nate needed money for a combine harvester and wanted to create a co-op of local farmers who would share machinery. It was a fantastic concept, and it would benefit a lot of farmers in the area. Angela inwardly cursed herself. She'd been so involved in her own problems that she hadn't realised, or even thought to ask, what anyone else around her might be going through.

While Lauren provided her thoughts on the idea, Angela gathered up their dishes and met Beth in the kitchen.

'You didn't have to do that,' Beth said, wiping her hands on her apron. Angela placed the dishes on the steel bench next to the sink.

'It's okay. I needed a breather,' she said.

'Everything alright?'

'Yeah. I just realised how bad a friend I am.'

Beth scoffed. 'You are not. You've had a lot going on lately, that's all.'

'But other people have too, and I've been too wrapped up in myself to notice.' Beth looked past her to where the others still sat talking.

'I reckon you've got some good people around you who don't mind about that.' Angela glanced back at the table. Adam was saying something. The rest of the group burst into laughter. Those people out there were her friends. Heck, they were almost family. If they had an issue with her behaviour, they would tell her. The only one who might not, who was new to the fold, was Nate. But she had a feeling he was on her side too. And she vowed to repay his generosity in any way she could.

Chapter 9

Charlotte slowly ran her fingers across the top of her mother's jewellery box. The tinny tune she'd heard almost every day of her childhood echoed in the room. Pulling out one of her mother's gold necklaces, she held it up to her neck and looked in the mirror. Angela's features were more like their mother's. Hers was a mixture of both her parents—her dad's eyes and chin, her mum's nose and mouth. Charlotte sighed and put the necklace on top of the chest of drawers.

'You can take that if you want. I'm sure Mum would have wanted you to have it,' Angela said.

Charlotte turned to face her. 'But if it's worth something, we should sell it.'

'If you want it, Lottie, take it. I want us to keep the things that really mean something to us rather than holding onto random stuff because we think we should.'

Charlotte picked up the necklace again. It was her mother's favourite, and now it would be hers. She rummaged in the jewellery box and held up a pair of earrings to Angela.

'You always loved these,' Charlotte said.

'I loved them on Mum,' Angela quipped. Charlotte sucked in a breath and moved to put them in the sell pile. 'But yes, I'd like them. Thank you for thinking of me.' Angela held out her hand, and Charlotte dropped the earrings in.

A car horn tooted, and they went outside to greet the potential buyers of the spare car. They'd stopped calling it "Mum's car" when they had decided to sell it. The older couple had driven up from Mullewa to view it. The woman got out, and Charlotte was pleased to see she sported a blonde bob, much like her mother's. After the introductions, she stood back and let Angela handle the transaction, but when the woman started to drive down the driveway, Charlotte moved next to Angela. Her stomach churned, and she swallowed hard. When the car was no longer in view, she turned and buried herself in Angela's shoulder, sobbing.

It had been months since their parents had passed away, but some days it still didn't feel real. Charlotte often felt like her mother was going to walk through the door at any moment and announce that she was going to make a tiramisu or a batch of coleslaw as a side to her dad's BBQ skills. When Charlotte realised the reality of the situation, she felt the loss anew. She wondered how long it would feel like that and whether her life would ever feel normal again. She opened her mum's side of the wardrobe, pulled the coat hangers out, one by one, and threw the clothes onto the bed. Neither of them would fit their mother's clothes, so they'd need to be donated to the op shop at the Community Resource

Centre. She reached up to pull down the boxes that were spread across the top shelf. The last box was tucked deep in the back corner. Spotting a stepladder, she climbed up to reach it.

'Want a coffee?' Angela asked from the doorway. Charlotte jolted and fell back, tumbling to the floor, the box landing open on her lap. Angela gasped. Charlotte looked from her to the contents now spread across her midsection—folded paper, some mementos they'd given their mother on Mother's Day, and most surprisingly, money in all denominations.

'What the heck? Why was Mum hiding all this cash?' Charlotte asked. Angela shrugged and then bent down to gather and count it. Charlotte unfolded the letter. It was addressed to them both. She read it aloud.

'Dear Angela and Charlotte,

If you're reading this, then it means I'm not here anymore. I'm so sorry to have left you both. I want you to know that you were the best thing to ever happen in my life, and I loved you immensely.

You're probably wondering about the money. You might recall that I always said a woman should have money "just in case." This is my just in case money. Just in case something happened to your father or between your father and me. Just in case something happened to you. Just in case I needed it.

Since you're reading this, I guess I haven't needed it. I hope it will come in handy for you both now. Please spend it. Save your own money for "just in case" and use this money for something that will help you both.

And please don't spend too long grieving. Remember all the wonderful things we did together. Remember our family holidays. Remember cooking up a storm and getting covered in flour. Remember all the board games and card games. Remember the fun we had. I remember it all, and I am so glad that I got to do it with you.

Love always,

Mum.'

Silence permeated the room, broken only when a sob escaped Charlotte's lips. She couldn't hold it in. Bent double with grief, chest heavy, tears streaming down her face, Charlotte cried for the past and the future. A future that would not be the way she wanted it to be.

She felt Angela's arms around her, and they sat unmoving for a long time. Eventually, Charlotte took a deep breath. She wasn't ready to put her feelings into words, so instead she gathered up the money and began counting it. When she was done, she realised that her mother's "just in case" money was just the thing to help them out of their precarious situation. Their mother's final act of love would help them to save their family home.

☆

Angela had called the bank to let them know the payment would be forthcoming. Adam and Lauren needed to fly back to Perth, so the trip to Geraldton was bittersweet. The hours flew by as they discussed the station stay, but it didn't take Adam long to turn the conversation to Nate.

'Ang, I know things with Andy didn't go the way you wanted, but maybe there was a reason for that,' Adam said.

'Are you getting philosophical on me?' Angela asked. Adam scoffed.

'Never. I just think you should see where it goes.' Angela shrugged. Maybe she would. But a relationship was not her top priority at the moment. That honour went to saying goodbye to her friends and then heading to the bank. She waved as they ascended the stairs and disappeared into the aeroplane. Their stay had been brief, but it had given her the spark she desperately needed. And they'd vowed to come back if she needed help with the station stay. She had promised they could be the first guests.

The queue at the bank was short. Angela had felt nervous carrying a large amount of cash in her handbag. What if she somehow lost it between home and the bank? What if someone robbed her? It wasn't likely to happen, but that didn't stop the intrusive thoughts.

The young teller called her forward. She explained the situation, and the teller nodded, clearly unconcerned about how stressful the situation had been for Angela and Charlotte. Angela thought about her parents. They'd taken out the loan to help Charlotte. They would have done the same for her. But they hadn't banked on a bad year with the sheep. It wasn't their fault. If it weren't for the accident, they would have paid off the loan, and nobody would have known. Only, it hadn't happened that way. Angela and Charlotte had been dealt blow after blow. Angela thought back to her mum's letter. She'd had "just in case" money ever since she'd earned enough to actually save instead of living paycheque to paycheque. It had created the safety net that her mum wanted. And now, her mum's safety net was helping her.

Handing the cash over and taking the receipt felt anticlimactic.

'Thank you. This puts you ahead on the loan schedule. The bank will expect the remainder to be paid out on time,' the teller said, then looked past her to the next person in line.

Angela walked to the foreshore, pulled her phone out and called Charlotte.

'It's done.'

'Woo-hoo! That's such a relief,' Charlotte said. 'You know, I'd totally forgotten about Mum's little speeches. Remember how many times she told us we could do anything we set our minds to?'

'Yeah. I really miss her.'

'Me too,' Charlotte said, sucking in a breath. Angela kept her eyes glued to the waves. She didn't want to dissolve into tears in public.

'We've got some leeway now, but we still have to focus on paying the loan off in full. We'll get there. I'll see you tomorrow.' Looking out at the choppy ocean, Angela felt the salty breeze on her face as a weight lifted from her body.

Nate watched Angela's face as the buzzing overhead drew her eyes up to the drone making its way across the clear blue sky. A smile broke out, and Nate felt a now-familiar pang in his chest.

'What do you reckon?' he asked. 'Shots across the paddocks towards the Ridge. Then a few facing back towards your place. Maybe some video of the sheep running in the paddocks?'

'Sounds good.' Angela beamed and stood next to him, looking up. 'It's the perfect day for it.'

Attempting to concentrate on controlling the drone, Nate acutely felt her presence next to him. His skin tingled as they stood together and watched the drone fly across the cloudless sky. Angela tilted her head and, before long, was directing Nate on where she thought the best photos would be taken. He didn't mind; she was the marketing guru after all. When they'd decided they had enough footage, they headed to the back verandah.

Nate set his laptop up on one side of the table, and Angela set hers on the other. While he waited for the footage to download, he made them both a drink and found some muffins in the cupboard. He'd spent so much time here when Jack and Susan were alive that it felt like a second home. He set the cups and food down and took his seat as Angela shifted her laptop so that he could see the screen. A professional website popped up, announcing Ridgeview Station Stay would be opening soon.

'What do you think?' Angela asked. He clicked through the website and then back to the homepage.

'This is awesome. Did you do all this yourself?'

A blush of pink bloomed across Angela's cheeks. 'Yeah. I like a challenge. Once we get your photos and videos up, it'll look even better. I can hold off on the accommodation photos until everything's finished. But this is the part I really enjoy, so I wanted to get a head start on it.'

'With a website like that, I reckon you'll have your first customers booked in before we've even finished setting everything up.'

'I hope so. Now, we've got to actually build the accommodation. I'm heading to the Shire office today to sort out the approvals.' She crossed her fingers.

'It'll be fine. I can't see why they'd object. We'll have this all up and running in no time.' He would make sure it was.

'Same with your co-op too, I hope.'

'Yep. We'll both be entrepreneurs,' he said with a wink, noticing the slight dip of her mouth before she smiled. 'Speaking of that, I think we need an extra set of hands,' he said. Angela tilted her head, and a look that Nate couldn't place crossed her face. 'There are a couple of young blokes on the footy team who wouldn't mind a bit of work.'

'Sounds like a plan,' she said. Nate grinned. He'd already lined up some farmhands, and he'd spoken a few times with Lauren since she and Adam had returned to Perth. The co-op could work with the right systems in place and the right people on board. Now, he just needed to get the ball rolling.

Angela and Charlotte, who was there for moral support, sat in the swanky waiting area of the new Shire office. The building looked out of place in Sanderson Ridge. The glass frontage and steel and brick façade screamed at rather than welcomed anyone who walked past it. The waiting room chairs were uncomfortably rigid, and the industrial-style coffee table plonked in the centre sat heavy and foreboding. Angela's stomach churned. She'd downloaded the forms off the shire's website and filled them in. There didn't seem to be any glaring problems. Surely the shire would approve her proposal. Having a station stay in the town would be good for tourism. It could boost the shire's profile without them lifting a finger or opening their purse.

A man with thinning white hair and a faded grey suit introduced himself as Simon Granger and ushered them into his cramped office. His face gave nothing away as he sat across from them and clasped his hands together on the desk. Angela pushed the paperwork towards him.

'I think this should all be in order,' she said. He scanned the documents and raised an eyebrow. Angela's foot began tapping softly. If this man didn't approve their permits, then she'd never see her idea come to fruition. After what seemed like half an hour but was probably only five minutes, Simon looked up with his mouth set in a thin line. Angela's heart sank.

'This isn't something I've dealt with before. I think it will need to be approved by the CEO and potentially the council. It's going to take some time.'

Angela's shoulders slumped. *Of course,* she thought sarcastically. Nothing ever happened quickly in Sanderson Ridge.

Charlotte let out a frustrated groan. 'How long?'

Simon shrugged. 'As long as it takes. In the meantime, I suggest you sit tight and wait.' Angela could feel the frustration emanating from Charlotte, and she put a hand on her arm to stop her protesting. It wouldn't do them any good to get this man offside. She stood and reached a hand out across the desk.

'Thank you. We look forward to a quick resolution on this,' she said as they shook hands.

Angela and Charlotte walked up the road to the general store in silence. Kane was in the yard sorting through some bags of fertiliser. He looked up as they approached.

'Well, from the looks on your faces, I'd say it didn't quite go as planned.'

'Not quite,' Angela said, shaking her head. 'Standard procedure, I guess, but it could take a while for approvals to come through.'

'Bugger,' Kane said.

'Surely, he could have approved it? We can't do anything now,' Charlotte said, kicking a bag of fertiliser.

'There's nothing we can do about it. We've got to let it go through the process. We might not be able to work on the accommodation, but we can get other things organised—fencing, driveways. We can finalise the look we want for the interior. That kind of thing.' Charlotte gave a lopsided smile. It wasn't ideal, but it was all they had to work with. The station stay would get approved eventually.

Angela looked at her phone and jolted. 'Come on, or we'll be late.' The two women walked to the edge of the footpath. Charlotte stopped mid-step to turn back.

'I'll close up the shop and meet you there,' Kane said. Charlotte bounced along the footpath towards the bakery. Balloons were strung across the chalkboard announcing its grand re-opening, which now, thanks to Charlotte's decorating and a rejig of the menu, was more like a café.

Angela was surprised to see a line of people waiting to enter the shop. They joined the back of the queue.

The façade had been painted to look like a retro diner. Black and white checked pattern covered the bottom quarter of the building, red and teal paint covered the rest, "Beth's" emblazoned in large black letters across the window. The proprietor herself was making her way down the line, thanking everyone for coming along and assuring them she'd be opening soon. She clicked her tongue when she saw Charlotte.

'What are you doing back here? I didn't want to open up without you. You've done all the hard work after all. Come on.' Beth dragged Charlotte, who grabbed Angela's arm and pulled her along. As soon as they reached the front of the line, a cheer erupted. Beth raised her hands to quiet the crowd. She encouraged Charlotte and her newly hired café all-rounder, 17-year-old Lara, to stand next to her before launching into her speech.

'Thank you all for coming today. It means so much to see so many people here. I know your usual stop-ins at the bakery have been interrupted for some time now, but trust me, it's all been worthwhile. I asked Charlotte to spruce up the bakery, but she's done much more than that. She's recreated it. Welcome to Beth's!' The crowd cheered as Beth turned around and cut a ribbon that had been strung across the front door. She turned back and embraced Charlotte, beaming and blinking back tears. Then they both pushed open the door and went in. The waiting crowd filed in, and soon enough, the café was packed tight with bodies, all admiring the new look.

Angela took in the booths by the far wall, the black and white checked floor tiles, the retro posters of old-time drinks and cars, and the new teal and pink fluorescent lights above the menu. The place looked nothing like it had. Charlotte had completely transformed it into something out of a design magazine. Angela looked over at Charlotte, her mouth agape.

'Lottie, this looks amazing. Well done!' She pulled her into a hug. 'I'm so proud of you.' Charlotte couldn't wipe the smile off her face as person after person came forward and congratulated her on her amazing work. Angela felt a surge of pride mixed with a surprised jolt. She had no idea that Charlotte was such a talented interior designer. Guilt struck her as she thought back to the night Charlotte had called her after a few too many drinks. Charlotte's pent-up frustration had boiled over, and now Angela could see why she'd been so upset. If Angela had stayed and Charlotte had left, she'd probably be a sought-after designer by now. She could have been travelling the world designing for an international clientele. Instead, she'd stayed in Sanderson Ridge after Angela left because she'd felt she needed to.

Beth and Lara handed out free samples of muffins and cakes. Charlotte moved behind the counter to help with sales. This wasn't the right time to talk to her. Was it worth rehashing it all anyway? She couldn't change the past. Angela smiled at Charlotte, then pointed out the door and waved. The official opening of Beth's was a success. It was great to see changes like this happening in Sanderson Ridge. She really hoped her station stay could be the next big change.

SPRING

"Spring: a lovely reminder of how beautiful change can truly be."

Unknown

Chapter 10

The sun warmed Angela's back as she stood to the side of the saleyards. The crowd was a sea of hats and checked shirts; everyone was buzzing with anticipation, including Angela. The truck had backed into the paddock early this morning, and Nate, Tom, and the new farmhand, Zac, had helped her load the lambs into the back. There were some wonderful moments in farming, like helping the ewes to give birth, but one of the hardest was hearing the sorrowful bleats as their lambs were taken away from them. Angela shuddered at the thought. Tom nudged her and nodded to a group of men standing with the auctioneer. Richard was holding court, and when he noticed Angela watching, he dipped his hat, a sly grin spreading across his face. Angela's gut instinct churned a warning.

Standing on the lowest rung of the fence, she leant over and checked the pens to find her lambs. Spotting them, she relaxed and waited as the auctioneer began calling for bids. The minutes seemed to pass incrementally. Nobody made a sound or lifted a hand. No bids meant no sales. Angela glanced up at Tom, whose brow was knitted together, and he leaned towards the man next to him, whispering. The auctioneer tried again. No luck. Angela looked around and locked eyes with Richard. He made a show of looking around and lifting his hands in surprise. Angela felt a surge of anger coursing through her. She pushed through the crowd to stand next to the auctioneer and made eye contact with as many men as possible. When the auctioneer called for final bids, she heard a cough from the back and saw a hand raise. She stood on her tiptoes to see who had saved her and was greeted with Nate's sheepish grin. A second later, another hand flew up, and then another. The bidding that had started slowly finished with a flourish. The ultimate sale price was more than she'd hoped. Relief flooded her, and she shot a look up to the cloudless sky.

'That was a close one,' a man's voice said. Angela felt a shiver run down her as she noticed Richard standing next to her.

'The end result is all that matters,' she said, hands on her hips. He shrugged a shoulder and turned to walk away. 'I could report you, you know.'

'For what?' he said, feigning ignorance. Angela shook her head, eyes fierce.

'You didn't win the farm, and you didn't win this auction. Why don't you just move on?' Richard let out a low laugh.

'Why would I do that? I'm having fun,' he said, then walked away laughing. Angela clenched and unclenched her fists. She closed her eyes and breathed deeply. Why did she let him get under her skin? She opened her eyes to find Nate standing in front of her, his face full of concern. He tilted his head and raised his eyebrows.

'Don't worry about it,' Angela said. 'Let's get out of here.'

The drive back to Sanderson Ridge was quiet. Tom kept his focus on the road, and Nate had his earbuds in. Angela looked out the window. The sale had gone well, but Richard's interference had rattled her. Still, she'd won this round, and she'd win the next one too.

Running back across the oval, sweat dripped down Nate's brow, and he wiped it away with the back of his hand. A hand slapped him on the back, and he felt an arm around his shoulders. The footy team gathered in a circle and sang the club song to the raucous applause of the spectators. They'd won the game, but a fall from a high mark had taken the wind out of Nate. He flinched and made his way over to the clubrooms. Someone called out, and he looked up to find Shane McGregor standing in front of him, grinning.

'Bloody good game. I would have played if it wasn't for this,' he said, lifting his arm, which was wrapped in a sling.

'Shame. How'd that happen? I've been meaning to catch up with you for weeks.'

'Hit a ditch and fell off my quad. I reckon I'll be off for the rest of the season. I wanted to have a chat with you too.' He pointed towards the carpark, and Nate followed him. The high from the win quickly deflated as he considered what Shane might have to say. Did he not want to be involved with the co-op anymore? It would never work without Shane's buy-in. He was born and bred in the Ridge. He had more clout around here than Nate ever would.

They fell into step and walked around the back of the carpark, as far from the clubrooms as possible. Nate couldn't wait any longer. He stopped and faced Shane.

'Do you want to back out of the co-op?' Nate blurted.

Shane's brow furrowed, and he shook his head. 'What? No, I was just wondering if you'd been to the Shire yet.'

'Oh, is that all? I was planning on heading in there on Monday.' At that moment, a car pulled up, and Will yelled out the window, 'Drinks at the pub. You coming?' Shane and Nate gave him a thumbs-up.

The pub was packed. It always was after a game. It didn't matter who had won or lost. Spectators and players from both teams all headed to the Imperial for a couple of pints. Nate had showered at the clubrooms before heading over. The warm water had helped to ease the tension he felt from the fall he'd taken.

Now on his second beer, he felt a pleasant warmth spread through him. With one elbow resting on the bar, he let his gaze wander across the crowd, nodding as he locked eyes with a few people. He saw Jamie and groaned inwardly as she headed towards him. The woman couldn't take a hint. She sidled up and ordered a white wine, then looked up at him with a smirk.

'Nate. How are you?'

'Fine, thanks. You?'

'Fabulous.' She wore a Cheshire cat grin that made the hairs on the back of Nate's neck stand on end. 'I saw Angela in here a few weeks ago with her friends from Perth. She was getting quite cosy with that guy. From the looks that passed between them, I'd say they were more than friends. Such a shame. I thought something was going on between the two of you.'

Nate took a swig of beer and forced himself to look at Jamie. 'You wouldn't have a clue. Adam's gay. He told me so himself.'

Without missing a beat, Jamie said, 'Well, he would say that, wouldn't he? Especially if he wanted to keep their relationship a secret.' Nate rolled his eyes and looked back at the crowd. She couldn't be right. Men didn't claim to be gay when they weren't, but then again, he'd seen them together and assumed they were an item. His thoughts turned to the way Angela had looked at him when she'd visited his place—vulnerable and needing support. But there had definitely been a spark when their hands touched.

'You're dead wrong. Maybe if you stopped trying to cause trouble for other people, you'd find someone who actually wanted to date you.' He waited until he saw his words register, then he grabbed his beer and walked towards a group of his teammates playing pool. He shot a glance at Jamie, but she was already stalking out the door. If this didn't finally give her the hint, he didn't know what would.

Most mornings were the same for a farmer. Rising early to get started on the never-ending chores. Nate found it easier to get up when the weather was warming up. He finished his eggs on toast and then got changed out of his work clothes and into a pair of jeans and a button-up shirt. It wouldn't do to look shabby when he was heading to the shire office.

Pulling up outside, he spotted Richard's black 4WD. The shire office wasn't open yet, so Nate decided to grab a coffee from Beth's. He ran a hand through his hair and shoved his hat on as he made his way over. Movement caught his eye, and he glanced up the path that ran alongside the shire building to where Richard and another man were standing. Richard shook the man's hand and started walking towards his car. Nate averted his gaze, but Richard called out.

'I hear you've got a scheme in the works.'

Nate shifted his hat. 'No scheme. Just a plan to help some of the other farmers.'

'Well, it sounds like something I could get behind. You come to me if you need anything, okay?'

Nate would never accept help from Richard, but he felt compelled to nod. Richard got into his 4WD and sped off. The door to the shire office swung open, and a young woman dragged a potted plant into the sun. Nate helped her position it and then followed her inside.

'How can I help you?'

'I'm just after some planning advice.'

'Sure. I'll just get Simon.' Nate shook the man's hand and recognised him as the person Richard had been speaking with. They went into his office, and Nate discussed his idea. Simon was accommodating and gave him the numbers of other organisations that might be able to help. Nate left the office feeling optimistic. He was making headway with his co-op.

The clouds had cleared from the light shower overnight, and the sun was out in the cloudless sky. Charlotte and Angela sat on the bench outside the general store. She felt Angela move and opened her eyes just in time to see the mail truck pull up.

'Not much in this drop,' the driver said as he grabbed a bag.

'No worries,' Charlotte replied, taking the proffered bag.

She hauled it over her shoulder and headed into the store to start the sorting. Angela grabbed a handful of envelopes and began slotting them into the cupboard behind the counter that housed the mail cubbies. Charlotte's phone pinged with an email. As she started reading, a wide smile spread across her face.

'What are you smiling about?' Angela asked.

'Oh, nothing. I've just won an interior design competition. That's all,' Charlotte replied, holding out the phone. Angela's jaw dropped, then she beamed and hugged her.

'Lottie, that's awesome. Congratulations! I didn't know you'd entered a competition.'

'I didn't tell anyone just in case I didn't get a place.'

'Let's celebrate. Dinner at the pub tonight?' Angela said. Charlotte agreed and went to find Kane to tell him the news. She knew he'd be happy for her, but his reaction was better than she'd imagined. He picked her up and whirled her around the room, cheering as she giggled and wriggled out of his arms. She tried to suppress her excitement, but his next words floored her.

'I think you should start that interior design business. I know the Ridge is small, but maybe there's a way to do it online or something. Angela could help with a website and marketing.' Charlotte didn't want to admit that she'd already considered the possibility of running her own business. She'd put it out of her mind long ago. They'd bought the shop, then her parents had died. It was never the right time to even contemplate it.

'Do you think I can do it?' she asked.

'Of course. I'll support you however I can. And I reckon we need to celebrate this,' he said, pointing to her phone.

'Yep. It's sorted. We're all having dinner at the Imperial tonight,' she said, then pecked him on the cheek and floated back into the shop like the world had opened up to her for the first time.

Angela was still sorting the mail when she returned, and they worked to empty the bag quickly. Charlotte reached in to grab the last envelope bearing Angela's name and the shire's logo. She handed it to her, and Angela's hand trembled slightly as she ripped it open. Charlotte watched her face for a reaction, and she bit her lower lip when she saw Angela frown.

'They knocked it back,' Angela said.

'What? How? Why?'

'It doesn't give any details. This is so unfair. There's nothing wrong with the documentation I submitted, and my business proposal is sound. I need to take this higher up.'

'Yes. You do,' Nate said. Neither of them had heard him come into the shop. He stood on the opposite side of the counter. He took off his hat and ran a hand through his fringe, raking it off his face.

'What do you mean?' Angela asked. Nate explained what he'd seen outside the shire office. The more he spoke, the higher the heat rose in Charlotte's face as the anger pulsed through her. She imagined Angela felt the same, and from the scowl on her sister's face, she was right.

'I can't believe he'd do this,' Angela said, huffing and shaking her head. 'I knew he'd try something when his stunt at the sheep sale failed.'

Nate jerked his head towards Angela. 'What stunt?'

'The radio silence during my auction was his doing,' Angela replied. Nate's face grew hard. Charlotte grabbed her phone and dialled the shire office. The receptionist was an old school friend who managed to slot them in for a meeting with the CEO later that afternoon. 'I'd better get home and spruce up the business plan. I want to get some stats on other station stays and tourism numbers,' Angela said, already heading for the door.

'Are you going to mention Richard?' Charlotte asked. Angela shook her head.

'Not if I don't have to. If we angled this the right way, the shire won't be able to refuse.' Charlotte hoped she was right.

Angela and Charlotte were barely in the waiting area for five minutes before the CEO came out to greet them. Laurence Hopkins was tall with a smattering of white hair along the sides of his head. His blue eyes were sharp, but the surrounding wrinkles belied his age. He had been a friend of their dads since they'd both attended primary school together. While Jack Martin always knew he was going to take over Ridgeview Station, Laurence Hopkins knew he'd own the biggest house within the town centre and follow in his own father's footsteps into local government. They shook hands, and he led them into his office. Situated at the front of the building, one wall was made entirely of glass windows, facing the main street. The other walls were lined with framed certificates, photos, and newspaper articles dating back years.

Angela and Charlotte sat in the plush winged chairs while Laurence took his seat behind the large oak desk that dominated the room.

'It's good to see you two again. How are you travelling? You know your dad was a good friend of mine.'

'I know. Thank you for the flowers, and please tell Mrs Hopkins that we appreciated the food she brought over,' Angela said.

'So what can I do for you?'

Angela sat forward and handed him a copy of her documentation, along with her business plan and the statistics that she'd found. She explained the situation, leaving out any mention of Richard. She didn't know how far Richard's influence went in the shire office.

'I think this could be a real boon for the shire. As you can see from the stats, these types of establishments have boosted tourist numbers in similar shires. The proposal was denied, but we believe there was no merit in that. We're asking for your approval. Once we have the go-ahead, we can have the station stay up and running within a matter of weeks.' Angela sat back and waited as Laurence read through the paperwork. She looked across at Charlotte, who sat biting her bottom lip, her face pale, and her fingers fidgeting with her wedding ring. Charlotte had a lot riding on this too. If the station stay was approved, Charlotte and Kane could focus on their shop. Charlotte had told her about her idea of starting an interior design business. It could happen, but it was all riding on a yes from the man in front of them.

Laurence read through the documentation, his head nodding slightly. Angela tried to steady her breathing. The wait was excruciating. She didn't have the patience for it. Finally, Laurence made a low, thoughtful hum and faced the two women.

'The application is sound. The marketing plan is detailed, and these statistics are impressive.' He sat back in his chair and ran a hand along his chin. 'Why do you think it wasn't approved?' Angela shot a look at Charlotte. Should they tell him what had happened, or would he think it was petty to tattle? Or worse, would he take Richard's side? Was he on Richard's bankroll like some others in town seemed to be? While Angela was considering the best approach, a Willy Wagtail landed on the windowsill, swishing its tail back and forth. Her breath caught in her throat. She'd read somewhere that the little black and white birds are sometimes thought to be visits from loved ones who had passed on. Perhaps this was a sign from her parents. She cleared her throat and brought her eyes up to meet Laurence's.

'Mr Hopkins—'

'Please call me Laurence.'

'Laurence. Not long after our parents' accident, Richard Kellerman approached me wanting to buy Ridgeview Station. I refused. He made several attempts at persuading both myself and Charlotte to sell.' Laurence's face gave nothing away, but Angela persevered. 'When it was clear that we were keeping Ridgeview, I believe he made an attempt to influence the decision not to grant approval for the station stay.' Laurence folded his hands on the table in front of him and looked from Angela to Charlotte.

'You understand that you're implying there's corruption within this organisation.' Angela swallowed the lump in her throat and nodded. Charlotte fidgeted with her wedding ring. Angela felt the magnitude of what might happen next. Laurence looked back at the paperwork, tapping a finger on the desk. When he looked up, his face held a grim smile.

'Thank you for your honesty. However, I can't approve this without conducting a formal review of the process that was undertaken by my staff.'

Charlotte sucked in a breath, and Angela's body went rigid. Of course, Laurence had to follow due process. There were laws about planning and anti-corruption at all levels of government.

'Your parents were always honest. It's wonderful to see that trait has passed down to the two of you. I hope that this review enables your business to be approved,' Laurence said, leading them out of his office. Angela felt deflated. She'd hoped a meeting with the CEO would solve her issues.

'Well, it wasn't a no,' Charlotte said.

'But it wasn't a yes.' Angela had to think. There must be something she could do. She walked back to her car parked outside the CRC building.

She hadn't been inside the building since it housed a short-lived dance school that she and Charlotte had attended for a term before the instructor moved back to Kellerberrin. The walls were covered with posters advertising online learning programs, government support, and health helplines. One room had been set up as a computer hub, and another held the clothes and bric-à-brac that formed the op shop. Angela found Mrs Higgins sitting at a small desk in a room off the galley kitchen. She looked over her glasses and stood.

'Angela, how are you? To what do I owe the pleasure?' Mrs Higgins said, indicating the chair opposite the desk. Angela sat and picked up the latest issue of the newspaper.

'You were a big help to me in high school when I couldn't grasp trig. Maths was never my strong suit. You were one of the best teachers I had.'

'Well, thank you. Flattery will get you everywhere.'

Angela smiled congenially. She needed community support. She'd stayed out of town until the effects of that damning letter had blown over. Now, she needed the newspaper to work for her, not against her.

'I'm thinking of starting a station stay on Ridgeview, and I was wondering if you'd like to run an article about it in the newspaper.'

'Well, this is a boon for our little paper,' she said, grabbing a notepad. She looked at Angela, eyes keen, pen poised. 'Tell me more.' Angela filled her in on her idea, slanting her angle to include the benefits to the town and omitting the failed application. If this went the way she hoped, it might help her application. Despite the processes the shire had to follow, the community still had sway in what went on.

'Thanks, Mrs Higgins. If you ever need me to take photos for the paper, let me know. I'd love to get back into photography. Time permitting, of course.'

'Of course, dear.' She looked down at her notes. 'I think I have everything I need. Be sure to check next week's edition.'

Kane laid the pancakes on their plates, and Charlotte added a smattering of maple syrup. She sat opposite Kane as he shoved a forkful into his mouth. They hadn't spoken about the potential business venture, but Charlotte had been laying the groundwork. She'd spent hours researching how to run online courses. She'd come up with a basic business plan. She even had a name for the endeavour—Lottie Designs. She eyed Kane. She knew by now that the best time to bring something up was when he had a full stomach.

'I've been thinking about this design business.' He looked up but kept eating. 'I'm going to go ahead with it.'

'That's great, babe. You're going to smash it' he said, grinning. Charlotte leant across the table and wiped a drip of maple syrup from his chin, then popped her finger into her mouth.

'Cor, don't get me started. We've got too much work to do,' Kane said. She winked, and they finished their breakfast quickly.

The bell above the door dinged. Charlotte glanced up to find Mrs. Higgins, her floral perfume preceding her, followed by Angela. The older woman deposited the newspaper onto the counter with a flourish. Angela grabbed a copy and held it up for Charlotte to see. The headline read "Sanderson Ridge: The new tourist hot spot" and featured a photo of Angela with the ridge in the background. Charlotte took the paper and read the article. Mrs Higgins had painted the station stay as a social and economic drawcard for the town.

'This is brilliant,' Charlotte said.

'Thank you. I trust this edition will remain on the counter,' Mrs Higgins said, eyebrows raised. Charlotte's cheeks burned.

'Of course it will,' Angela said. 'I hope everyone else in town thinks the station stay is a good idea.' Mrs Higgins nodded and left to drop newspapers at the other businesses. Angela turned to Charlotte. 'Ring me later and let me know if you hear anything.'

'Will do. I told Kane this morning.'

'That's great. I knew he'd be on board. That guy adores you.' Charlotte smiled but drew her lips into a thin line as Richard came into the store. Without glancing in her direction, he made a beeline for Angela.

'Well, it seems that you've created quite a stir with your article.' *That was quick*, Charlotte thought. In truth, it didn't surprise her that Richard was aware of the article. He was generous in his financial support of the CRC.

'In light of recent events, I just wanted to let you know that I have purchased the Johnsons' farm. Ridgeview Station wasn't big enough after all.' He pushed his shoulders back and puffed out his chest. Charlotte waited for the next jibe. Angela stood stock still as he continued. 'I'm a businessman. I saw an opportunity, and I attempted to take it. I was unlucky in this instance. But I'm glad to see you've got some grit and a head for business. Good luck with the station stay. Perhaps it'll start a trend.' He tipped his hat, then pivoted and walked out. Charlotte and Angela looked at each other in disbelief.

Angela's phone rang and broke the silence. Charlotte watched her face transform, the initial surprise replaced by a wide, excited grin. Angela shoved the phone into her pocket.

'That was Laurence. He wanted to give me a heads-up that the review's been finalised. I'll get the paperwork soon, but he wanted to let me know that my application's been approved.'

Charlotte breathed out. 'Finally!' Seeing the relief spread across her sister's face, tugged at her heart with a sharp pang. She reached over the counter and pulled Angela into a hug. 'Dinner at the pub tonight. We're celebrating!'

Chapter 11

Beer cascaded into glasses, laughter and music filled the air, and a sweet, intoxicating aroma hung around the room. The restaurant was at capacity, but the table Nate sat at seemed to be the loudest. Kit and Will sat opposite Charlotte and Kane, while Angela sat next to Nate. They were all there to belatedly celebrate Charlotte's win in a national interior design competition, and Angela's recent approval to set up the station stay. Nate coughed loudly to get everyone's attention.

'I've got a bit of good news myself.' He waited for a beat to build the tension, then he raised his glass. 'I've got the backers and support, so I'm going ahead with the co-op.' The group erupted in cheers, and drinks sloshed as they clinked.

'That's great news,' Angela said, leaning over and putting an arm around his back. Nate felt a tingle run through his body. He could smell her sweet, flowery perfume and feel her movements next to him.

'Thanks. I wouldn't have even tried if it wasn't for you,' he said. She tilted her head, and he continued. 'You made a decision, and you went for it. No doubts. No second-guessing yourself.'

Angela chuckled. 'Believe me, the thought that I might be making a huge mistake has crossed my mind so many times over the past few months.'

'Here's to new beginnings,' Nate said, raising his beer and gently clinking it with her glass. After the toast, he could barely pull his eyes away from hers until a group walked into the restaurant. Nate groaned, and Angela's face shot up to see who'd elicited that reaction. Jamie and Sam walked in on the arms of two Merredin football players. Angela bristled and shifted in her seat so that she wasn't as close to him. Jamie looked over and waved at them. Nate kept his face turned forward, expression neutral.

'Jamie told me you and Adam were a couple,' he said.

Angela choked on her drink. 'She what? Oh my god. I don't think Jamie's ever going to stop trying to make my life miserable. You didn't believe her, did you? I mean, you've met Adam. He's not into this.' She gestured to her body, and Nate tried not to follow its direction.

He let out a low laugh. 'Yeah. He didn't hold back when he told me about moving in with Ryan.'

'He's one of my best friends, but obviously, there's nothing going on there. Never has been and never will be.'

'Good to know,' Nate said. He winked at her and felt a now-familiar pang at her blush.

Hours later, the cook kicked the group out of the restaurant and into the bar. The music was thumping, but armed with liquid courage, Nate turned down the stereo. Shouts of 'Hey' and 'Oi' erupted from the crowd, but Nate raised his hands, and the grumbling settled down. All eyes were on him, and he momentarily regretted his decision.

'I know you want the music back on, but,' he pointed to his friends, 'we have something to celebrate. Well, three things actually. And I wanted to share the good news with you all.' He pointed to Charlotte. 'You've all seen the reno at Beth's, right? Well, that has won Charlotte a national interior design competition.' Everyone clapped and cheered. Charlotte beamed and mouthed thank you. Nate locked eyes with Angela, and she glared at him, but he kept going.

'And Angela, who thankfully decided to stay in Sanderson Ridge, is about to build the town's very first station stay. It'll bring tourists to the region, and that's something we can all benefit from.' Fewer cheers erupted, but the crowd still clapped. 'And as for me, well, I've got a new venture in the works that will benefit local grain farmers. If you're keen on hearing more about it, come and see me. Preferably when I'm sober.' The crowd laughed and applauded as Nate took a bow and started the music again. Wearing a wide, hopeful grin, he stumbled back to the others. Thankfully, he saw that Angela's expression mirrored his own. It was turning out to be one of the best nights he'd had in a long time.

The morning sun peeked through the curtains. Angela opened one eye and quickly squinted it shut. Her head ached, and her mouth was dry. She knew she'd pay for last night's antics, but she hadn't had a hangover like this since she was in her twenties. Groaning, she trudged to the kitchen to look for something to kill the aches. She looked out the kitchen window towards the ridge as she swallowed the tablets and downed a breakfast smoothie. A shadow caught her eye as it passed by the window. Moments later, there was a knock on the back door.

Angela checked herself and smoothed down her pyjamas, then tied her hair up before answering the door. Jamie stood on the verandah, eyes down. Angela's stomach churned, and she felt nauseous. Jamie had never been to her home before. She pulled open the door and ushered her in, bracing herself for bad news. Jamie looked around the room before settling her gaze on Angela.

'Can I help you with something?' Angela asked.

Jamie took a deep breath. 'I heard what Nate said in the pub last night. About the station stay.' Angela bit the side of her bottom lip. 'I think it's a great idea.'

Angela did a double take. 'You what?' Jamie shifted from one foot to the other, then cracked the knuckles on her hands.

'Look, I really came here to apologise. I've been a bitch to you lately. Well, for a long time actually.' Angela's eyebrows shot up and down. Jamie looked as nauseous as she felt.

'I could do with a cuppa. How about you?' she asked. Jamie nodded. Angela made small talk while she prepared the drinks.

'Thanks,' Jamie held the cup in both hands. 'I thought that since you're obviously staying here for good now, we should call a truce.'

'I never had any issues with you.'

'I know. It was all me. I started rumours about you and that thing with the newspaper,' she closed her eyes and shook her head. 'That was a bit childish. But I'm willing to put it all in the past if you are.' Angela thought back to high school and how much Jamie's bullying had affected her. She wasn't about to forgive and forget that easily.

'Do you have any idea what your words did to me? How bad you made me feel about myself? Geez, Jamie, I was so close to doing something terrible.' Jamie's face drained of colour.

'Oh my God. I didn't think...was I really that awful?' Angela nodded. 'I am so sorry. Really. I...' She looked down at the table and picked at her fingernails. Angela looked out the back door towards the ridge. Neither of them could change the past, so why dwell on it? She couldn't see the two of them ever being friends, but not being enemies sounded good to her. Smiling, she looked back at Jamie and lifted her cup in salute. Jamie did the same.

'So, this wouldn't have anything to do with that guy from Merredin footy club, would it?' Angela said with a smirk.

Jamie blushed. 'Maybe. He's thinking about moving here.' This change of heart felt surreal, and only time would tell whether Jamie was telling the truth or not. But now that the station stay had been approved, Angela had more important things to concern herself with.

The screen flashed as Charlotte shut down the laptop. She looked at her watch. It was almost midnight. She'd been tweaking the slides for her first webinar. With Angela's help, she bought the business name and insurance, created a website, and put an ad in the newspaper for the locals. Once she had the first webinar sorted, she'd advertise it everywhere she could think of. It had been a steep learning curve, but she'd enjoyed the challenge.

She gently lifted the doona and slipped into bed. Kane moaned and rolled over but didn't wake. Charlotte knew the alarm would go off in less than six hours, but she couldn't sleep. Ever since she'd started this business, her head had buzzed with ideas. She'd been sure to continue helping Kane with the store, but with John taking on more shifts, she could focus on her business.

She woke to an email from Grand Designers' magazine. They'd been one of the sponsors of the competition she'd won, and they wanted to feature her renovation of Beth's. This was going to help her business venture kick off with a bang. She moved her laptop to the spot she'd commandeered in the corner of the store and set to work again, a determined glint in her eye.

Angela's body tensed as Nate pulled the truck up and used the attached crane to winch the silo into position. Kit, Will, Tom, Charlotte, Kane, and Angela clapped as the metal hit the ground with a thud. Since their meeting with Laurence, Angela and Charlotte had finalised the interior design and ordered everything they needed. It had arrived quickly and was sitting on a pallet on the back of Kane's ute, ready to be unpacked and assembled once the silo was in situ. Nate had already sealed the inside and given the outside a few coats of rustproof paint. Now that it was in its final home, they had to start work on the interior. The plumber was scheduled to arrive the next day to connect the bathroom fixtures and the small kitchen sink, and the electrician would arrive the day after. The timeline was tight, but with this many helpers, Angela hoped they could pull it off.

She checked her clipboard and ran her finger down the schedule she'd created. The list of tasks seemed monumental, and she was nervous they wouldn't be completed on time. After doling out the jobs, everyone got to work. By lunchtime, Will, Kane, Tom, and Nate had constructed the second-floor mezzanine, and the ladder leading up to it had been set in place. Angela, Charlotte, and Kit had worked to unpack the pallet and lay everything out so that it was easily accessible. Angela left them to it and drove the ute back to the house to make lunch. Returning with a load of sandwiches, soft drinks, and flasks of coffee. She sat on the back of the ute and surveyed the progress, the sounds of hammering and sawing filling the air.

'It's coming along nicely,' Nate said as he hopped up and plonked down next to her. She felt his knee touch hers, and she didn't move it. Surreptitiously, she sniffed his aftershave, which was a heady mix of sandalwood and lavender that made her feel giddy. Smoothing down her shirt, she was glad she'd freshened up while she was back at the house.

'Yeah. I think we're more or less on track. I'll probably keep going until it gets too dark. Thanks for your help,' she said. Nate shrugged a shoulder, then gently placed his hand on her knee.

'Anytime,' he said. She felt heat rise in her body. Did he feel it too? They had almost shared a kiss after their celebratory night out, but he'd pulled back at the last minute. The next day, she was grateful for his chivalry. If she'd kissed him that night, she knew she wouldn't have been able to stop. But now, these subtle gestures revealed the depths of his feelings for her. And they felt right.

Kane approached the ute, and Nate shifted his hand.

'Shall we clock back on, boss?' Kane asked with a cheeky grin.

Angela laughed. 'Yeah. Get back to it or I'll crack the whip.'

The group pushed hard until five o'clock, then put down their tools, their work done for the day. Angela felt bad about keeping them there any longer. Thanking them all as they left, she stood in the paddock next to the now semi-completed silo accommodation. Her dream was finally coming together.

Nate lifted the toolbox onto the back of the truck and then walked back to where Angela stood. His body ached, and he longed for the quiet comforts of home, but he wasn't ready to leave her yet.

'We did a bloody good job. It looks shmicko,' he said. Angela giggled, and he felt a rush of warmth. The silo was now set up with a living space, a separate bathroom, and a small kitchen on ground level, and a bedroom that took up the entire mezzanine level. The basics were done, but there were a lot of finishing touches to go. 'Come on then. Let's see what else we can get done.'

'Don't you want to head home? It's been a long day.'

'Nah, I'd rather see this thing completed,' he said, jerking a hand towards the silo.

They worked together for another hour before the darkness halted their progress. Angela glanced up at the stars and the full moon. He noticed a shift in her mood but couldn't place its reason. They stood near the truck, and Angela looked back towards the Ridge. Nate moved closer, and as she looked up, he leant down, his hand sliding along the side of her neck and behind her head. He felt her stand taller and move closer until their lips touched gently. Nate's heart thumped, and his body tingled.

He stepped back and raised his hands. 'Sorry. I just...I—'

'It's okay,' Angela said, before rising onto her tiptoes to kiss him again, longer and more passionately. He reciprocated, then pulled away slightly so that their foreheads touched. Her hot, sweet breath hit him, and he felt his groin twitch.

'Are you sure about this?' he asked. He didn't want her to feel pressured into anything she didn't want to do.

'I'm absolutely certain. Are you?' she asked. He bristled. Was he? Did he want this? A memory of the first time he saw her popped into his head. She'd had an aura that was like a magnet to him. With sudden clarity, he realised he'd wanted to be with her from that moment.

'Yes,' he said, lightly resting his hands on her waist. He pushed her back gently and took a deep breath. 'There's something I have to tell you.' He felt her stiffen. 'I've been on my own for a long time. I was in a long-term relationship before I moved to the Ridge. It was all going well until I caught her in bed with one of my mates. My walls went up, and I thought I wasn't interested in dealing with all the stuff that relationships bring. Until I met you.' He felt her body relax in his arms, and he kissed her again, softly, then more passionately, not wanting to stop. Eventually, he pulled back.

'I'd better go. I'll be back first thing in the morning,' he said. He didn't want to go, but he also didn't want to rush this. He watched her in the rear-view mirror as he drove the truck down the driveway. Telling her about his ex was hard, but he needed to do it. Trust was a big issue, but after spending so much time with Angela over the last few months, he felt like she was someone he could put his trust in. He finally went to sleep late that night, utterly exhausted, his mind still buzzing with possibilities of the future.

Epilogue

One month later

Charlotte stood back almost on the road so that she could get a good look at the sign.

'A little to the left,' she called out to Kane. He shifted the heavy sign a few centimetres. 'Perfect.' Kane climbed down the ladder and put his arm around her waist, drawing her to him and planting a firm kiss on her lips.

'I'm proud of you,' he said, grinning at her. She hugged him again, and they walked back inside the store. Kane made his way to the shelves and started re-stocking the dry goods. Charlotte moved to the desk that now sat in the front corner. She turned on the laptop, opening up to her website where she would be hosting an online webinar in half an hour's time. She knew she'd be lucky to even have a few people attend, but it would be a start. She clicked on the link and watched as people entered the webinar and started chatting among themselves. She sat back in her chair, clasped her hands and brought them to her lips. It was go-time.

Kane waved to get her attention, and she took off her headphones.

'It's alright. The webinar finished a few minutes ago. I'm just monitoring my emails.'

'How did it go?'

'Good. I think. Everyone sounded really positive.' A message popped up, and she read it. 'Oh my God. I've got a client. My first actual client.' Kane pulled her to her feet and squeezed her. This was it. She almost pinched herself in disbelief. She was a fully qualified interior designer with her own business, and she'd achieved it all right here in Sanderson Ridge.

Angela waved at the young couple as they walked along the driveway back towards their accommodation. They had arrived earlier in the day, and Angela had greeted them with a bottle of wine, a box of crackers, and some locally made cheeses. They had already started taking drone footage and photographs to upload to their 100,000-strong following on social media. Angela had almost fallen out of her chair when the email came through asking if they could come and stay. With their influence, she had no doubt the one-bedroom silo and the new two-bedroom, tiny home would be booked out for weeks if not months in advance.

Nate was waiting on the verandah when she walked around the back of the house. She approached him and pecked him on the cheek before he handed her a drink. They made their way down to the dam and sat on the jetty with their own picnic of crackers and cheese. Angela took in the view of the sun setting on the ridge. This really was a magnificent place to live. She felt eyes on her and looked up into Nate's face. He laid his arm gently on her shoulders, and she put her arm around his waist.

'I'm so glad you stayed in the Ridge,' Nate said.

'Me too.' Another kiss and a sip of drink, and as the sun finally dipped below the horizon, she realised she was exactly where she was meant to be.

Also by Alicia Hitchcock:

Barbed Wire and Brumbies

Orange Sky: Sanderson Ridge Prequel

Courage and Dust (Coming 2026)

About the Author

Armed with an overactive imagination and a concerning amount of coffee, Australian author Alicia Hitchcock creates historical and contemporary novels filled with emotionally captivating drama, high-stakes tension, and heartfelt romance. When not travelling through time and space on the page, Alicia can be found exploring historical sites and modern cafés with equal enthusiasm.

Learn more at aliciahitchcock.com and connect with her on social media to keep up to date.

If you enjoyed reading this book as much as Alicia enjoyed researching and writing it, please hop online and post a review.